the MUTTS winter diaries ™

Other Books by Patrick McDonnell

Mutts
Cats and Dogs: Mutts II
More Shtuff: Mutts III
Yesh!: Mutts IV
Our Mutts: Five
A Little Look-See: Mutts VI
What Now: Mutts VII
I Want to Be the Kitty: Mutts VIII
Dog-Eared: Mutts IX
Who Let the Cat Out: Mutts X
Everyday Mutts
Animal Friendly
Call of the Wild
Stop and Smell the Roses
Earl & Mooch
Our Little Kat King
Bonk!
Cat Crazy
Living the Dream
The Mutts Diaries
Playtime

Mutts Sundays
Sunday Mornings
Sunday Afternoons
Sunday Evenings
Best of Mutts

Shelter Stories
A Shtinky Little Christmas

the MUTTS
winter diaries

· PATRICK McDONNEll ·

Andrews McMeel
Publishing®

Kansas City · Sydney · London

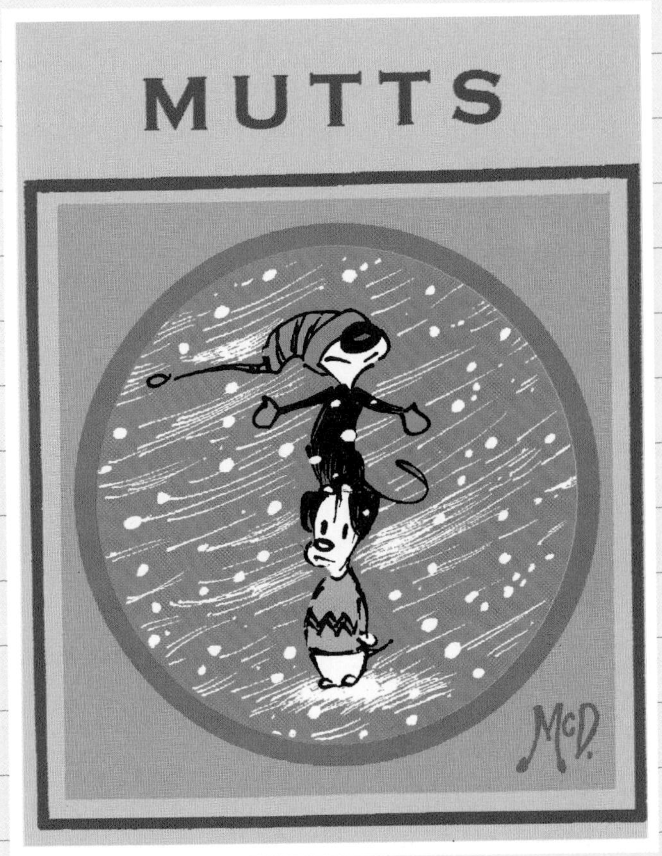
MUTTS
McD.

BRRR... IT'S COLD!
YESH
IT NEEDS TO BE TWENTY DEGREES WARMER
YESH
WHERE'S THE THERMOSHTAT AROUND HERE!?!

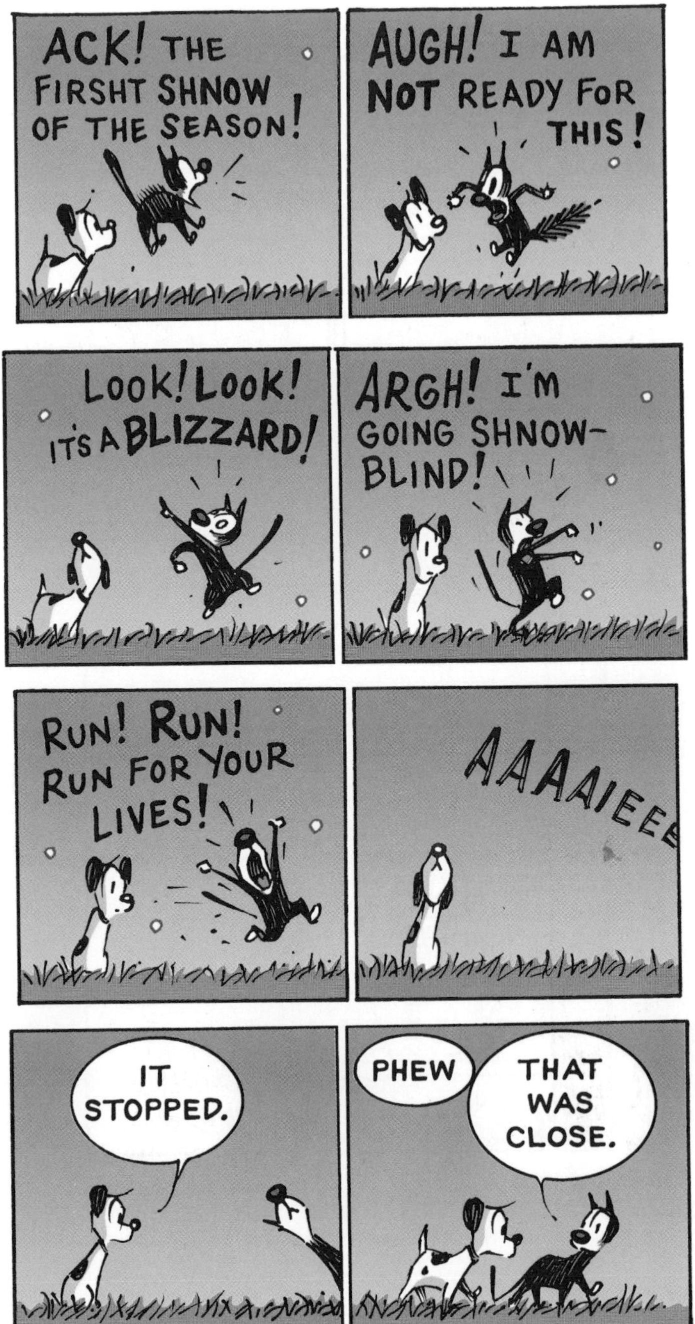
ACK! THE FIRSHT SHNOW OF THE SEASON!
AUGH! I AM NOT READY FOR THIS!
LOOK! LOOK! IT'S A BLIZZARD!
ARGH! I'M GOING SHNOW-BLIND!
RUN! RUN! RUN FOR YOUR LIVES!
AAAAIEEE
IT STOPPED.
PHEW
THAT WAS CLOSE.

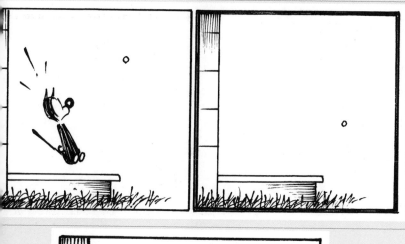

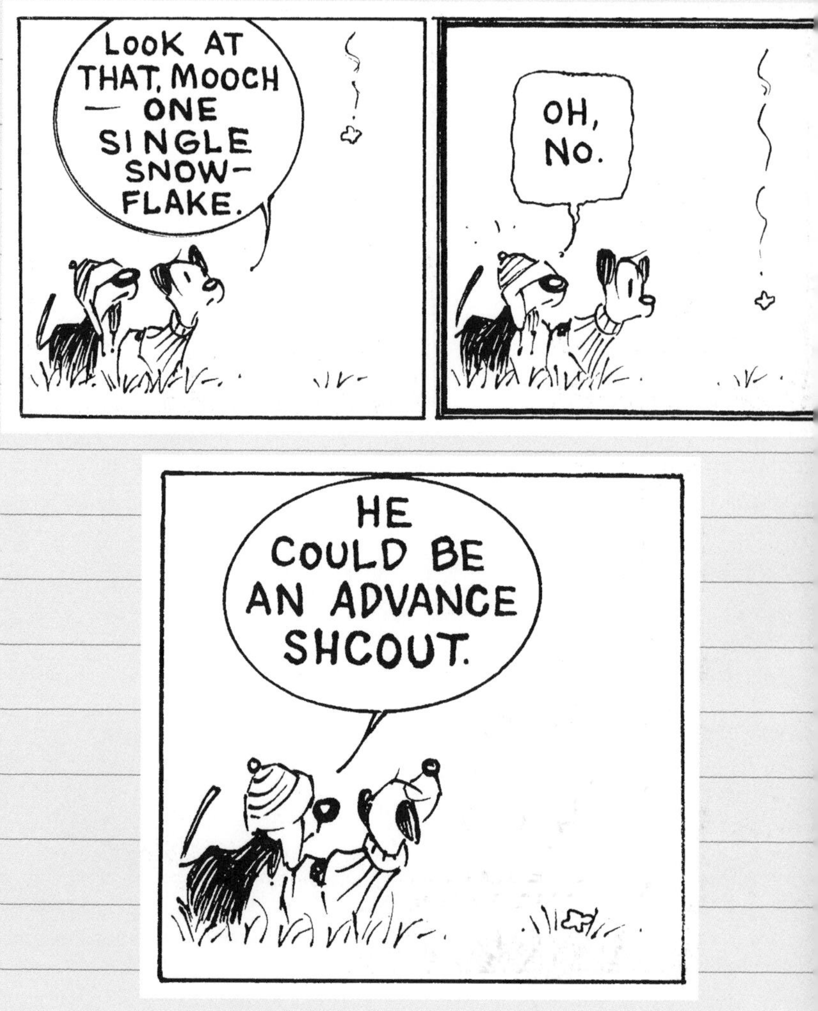
LOOK AT THAT, MOOCH — ONE SINGLE SNOW-FLAKE.
OH, NO.
HE COULD BE AN ADVANCE SHCOUT.

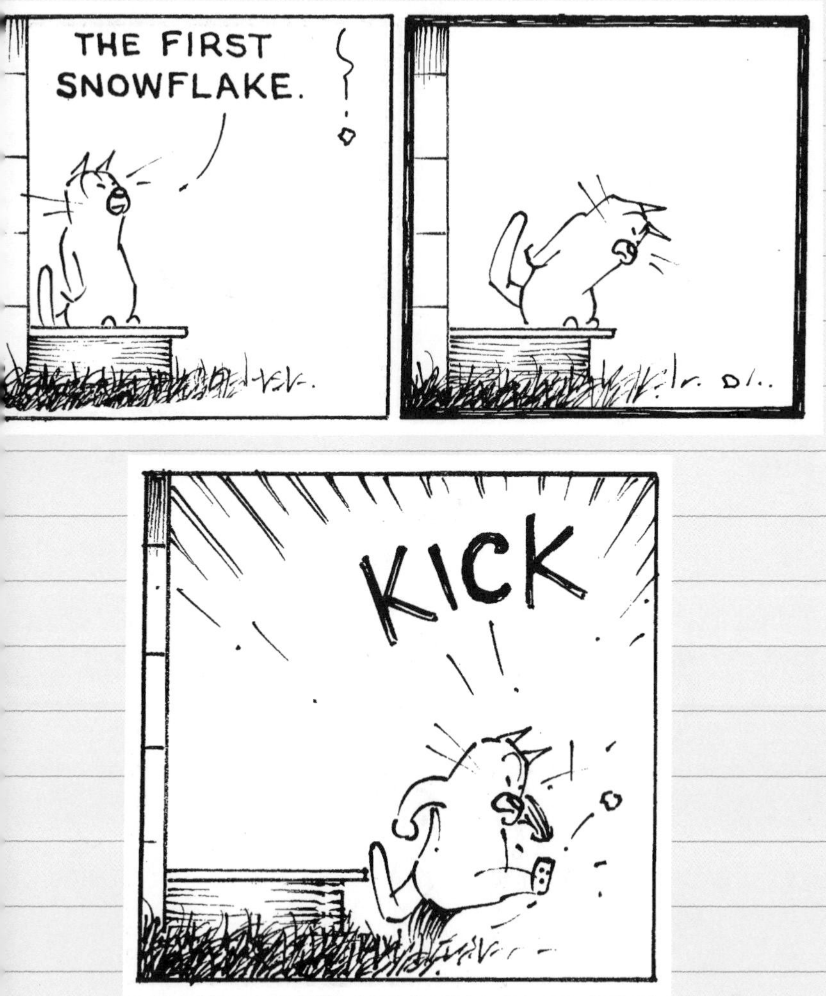
THE FIRST SNOWFLAKE.
KICK

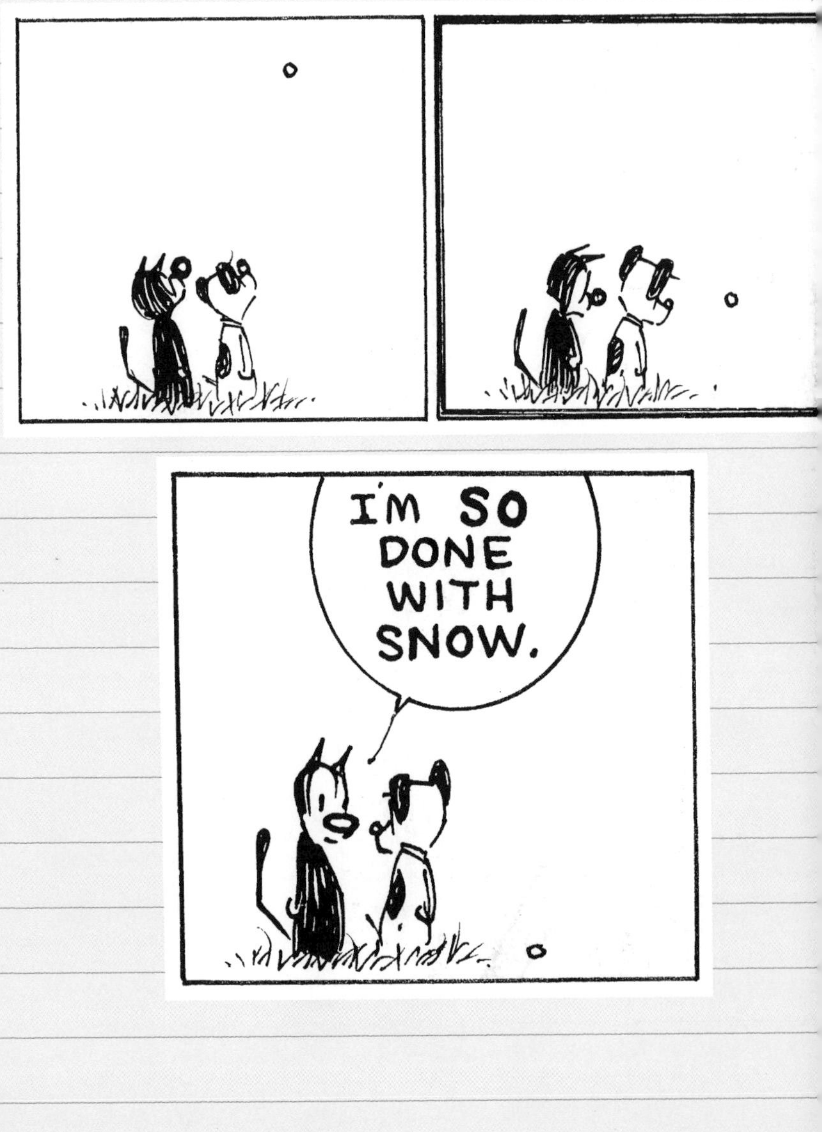
I'M SO DONE WITH SNOW.

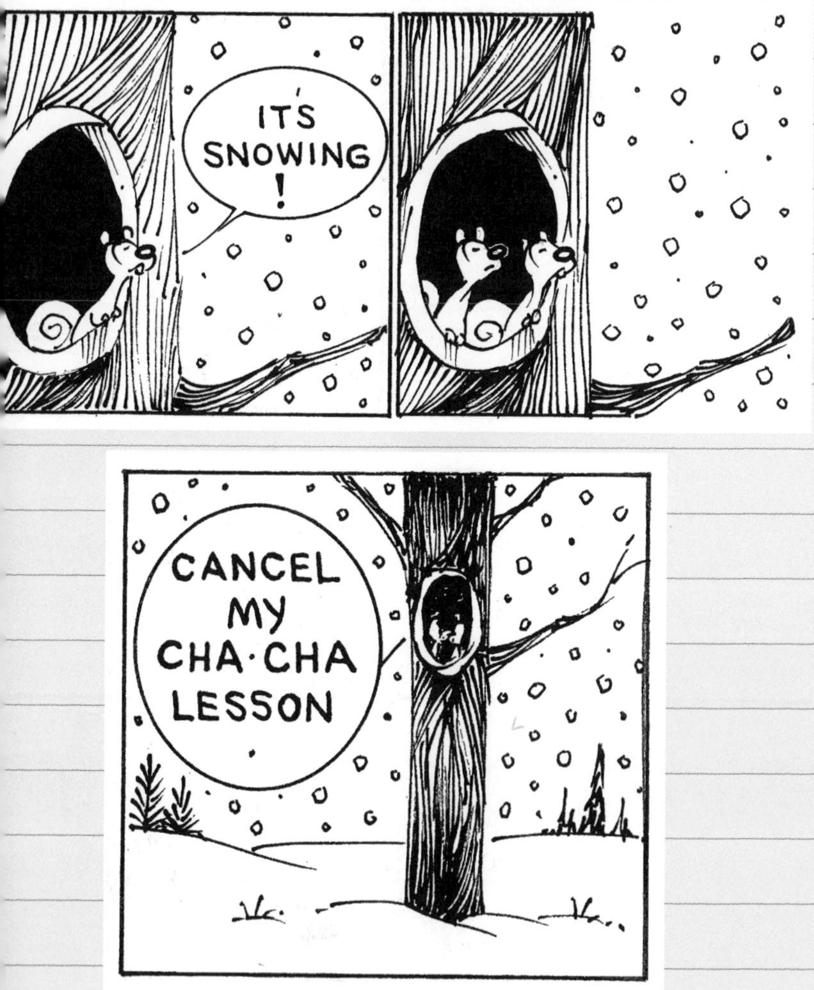

IT'S SNOWING !
CANCEL MY CHA·CHA LESSON

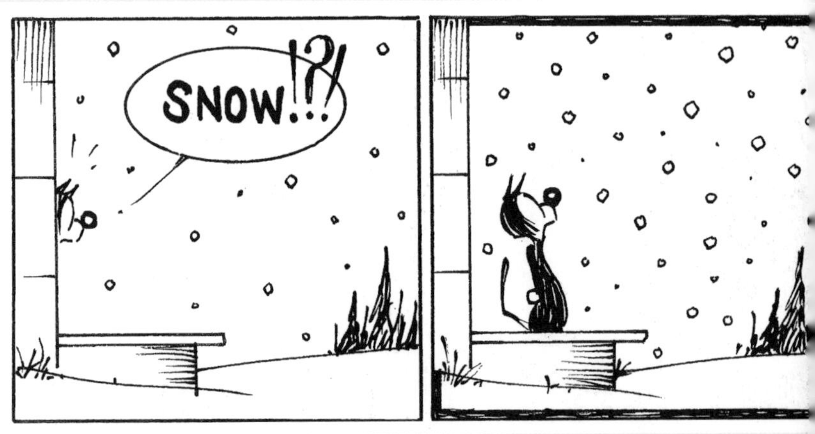
SNOW!?!

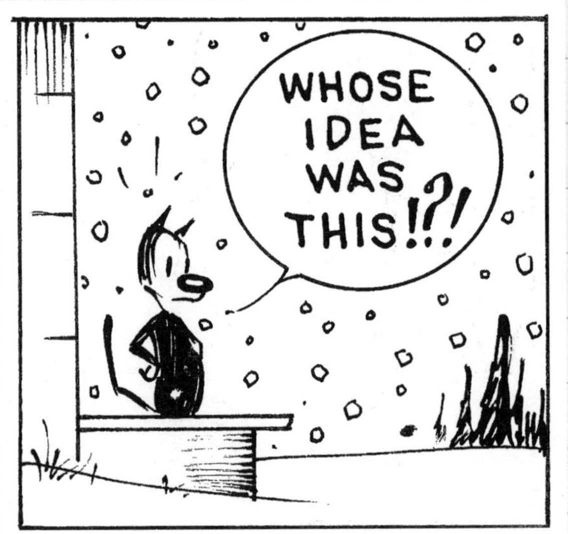
WHOSE IDEA WAS THIS!?!

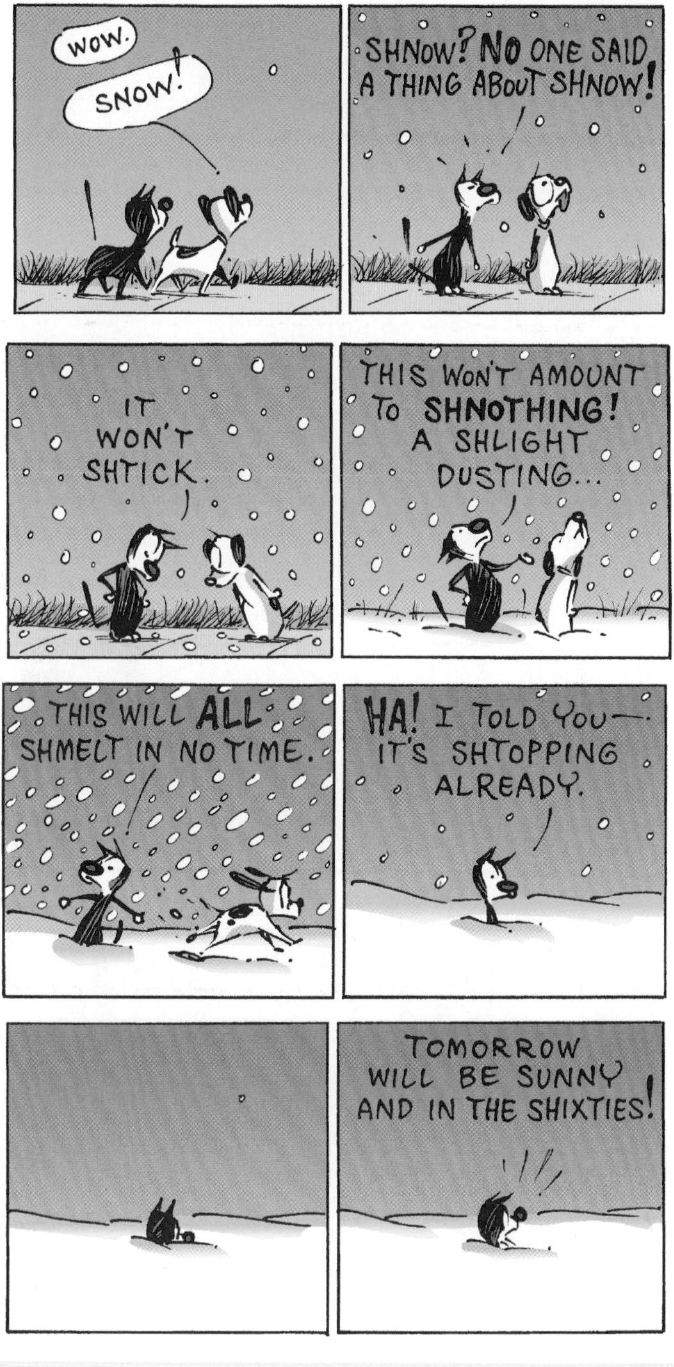
WOW.
SNOW!
SHNOW? NO ONE SAID A THING ABOUT SHNOW!
IT WON'T SHTICK.
THIS WON'T AMOUNT TO SHNOTHING! A SHLIGHT DUSTING...
THIS WILL ALL SHMELT IN NO TIME.
HA! I TOLD YOU— IT'S SHTOPPING ALREADY.
TOMORROW WILL BE SUNNY AND IN THE SHIXTIES!

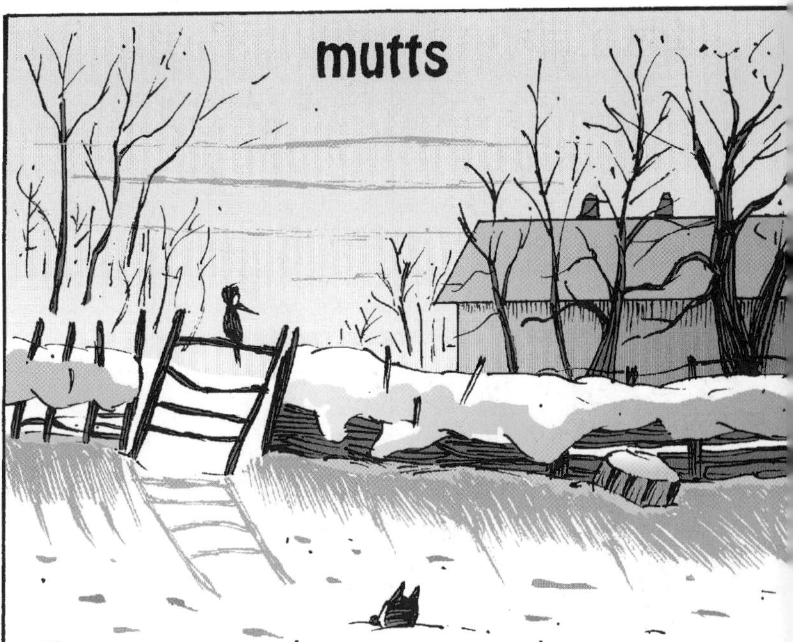
mutts

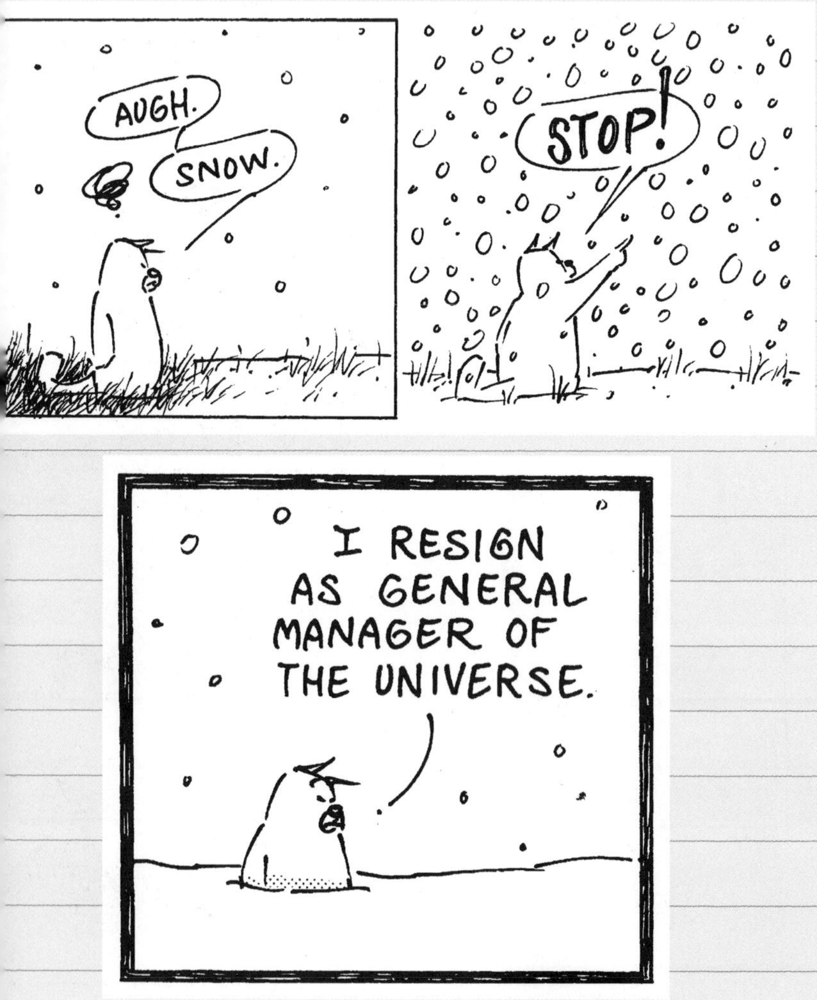
AUGH.
SNOW.
STOP!
I RESIGN AS GENERAL MANAGER OF THE UNIVERSE.

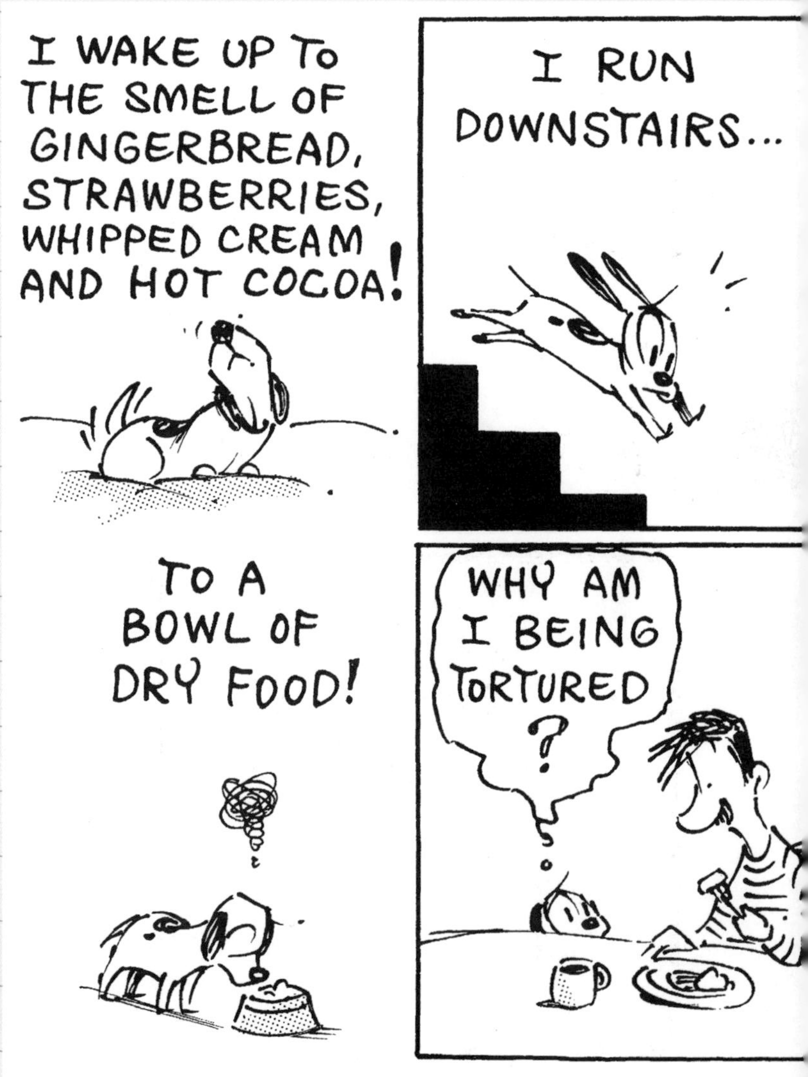
I WAKE UP TO THE SMELL OF GINGERBREAD, STRAWBERRIES, WHIPPED CREAM AND HOT COCOA!
I RUN DOWNSTAIRS...
TO A BOWL OF DRY FOOD!
WHY AM I BEING TORTURED ?

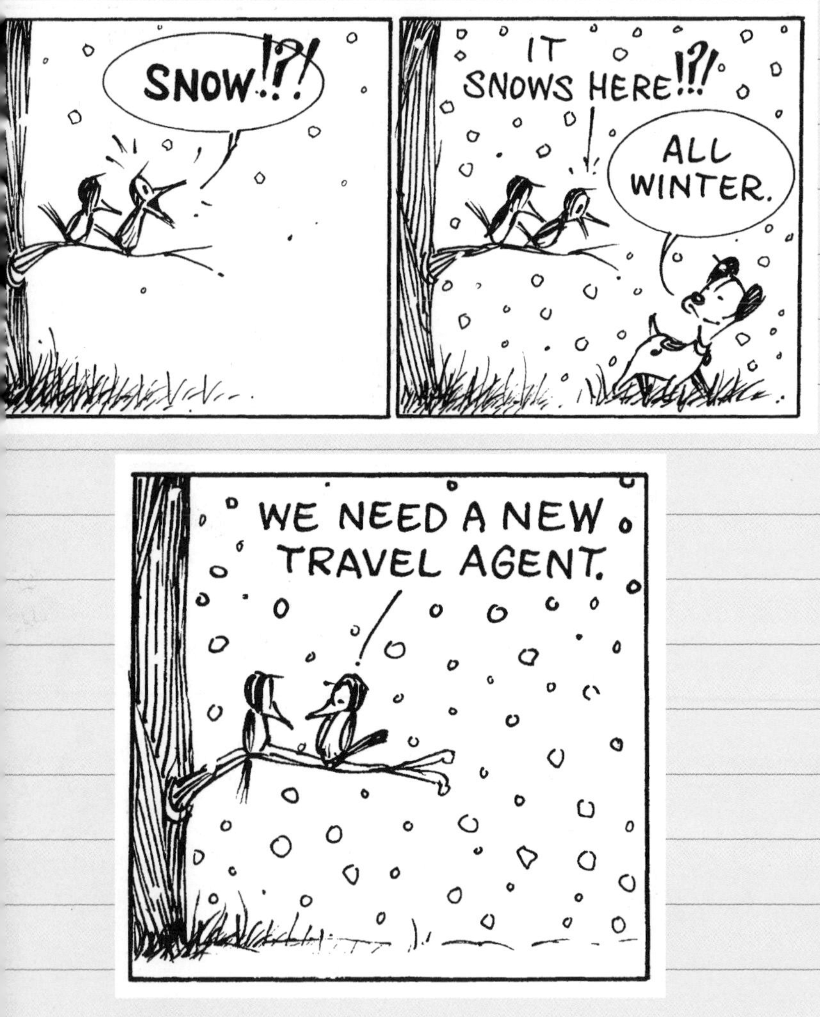
SNOW!?!
IT SNOWS HERE!?!
ALL WINTER.
WE NEED A NEW TRAVEL AGENT.

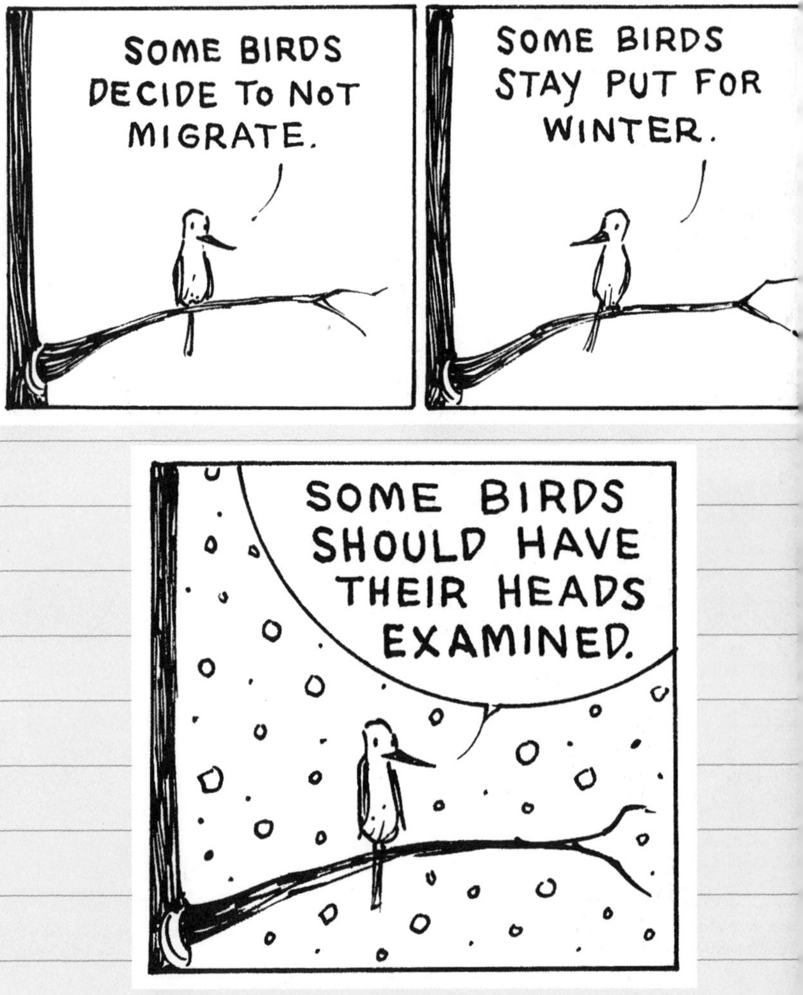
SOME BIRDS DECIDE TO NOT MIGRATE.
SOME BIRDS STAY PUT FOR WINTER.
SOME BIRDS SHOULD HAVE THEIR HEADS EXAMINED.

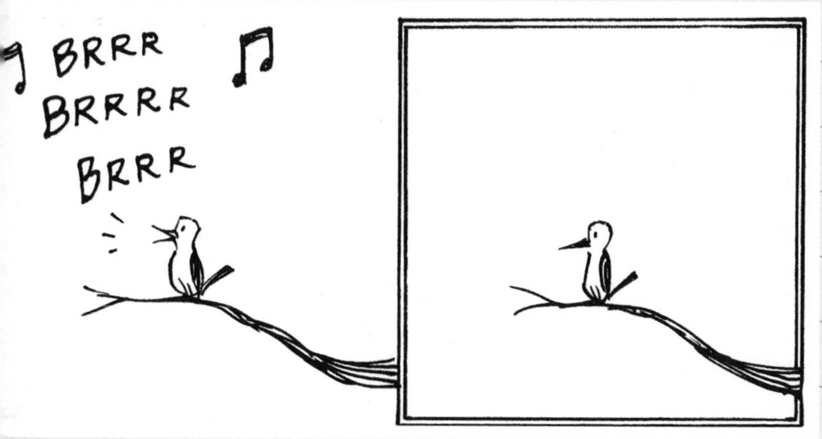
BRRR
BRRRR
BRRR

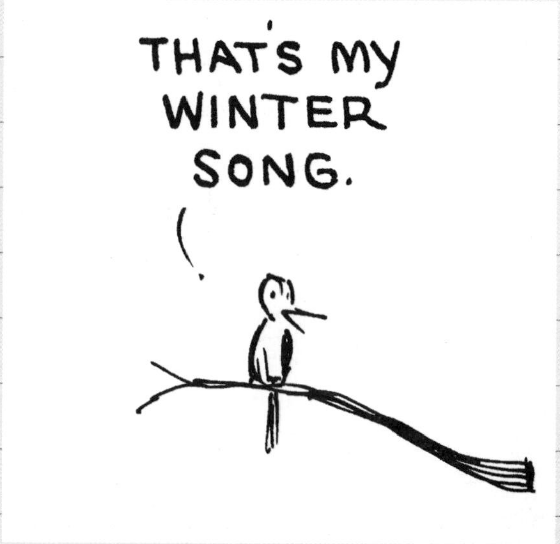
THAT'S MY WINTER SONG.

BIRDS FLUFF OUR PLUMAGE TO TRAP AIR TO CREATE A WARM INSULATING LAYER.
POOF
IT'S A LITTLE CHILLY TODAY.

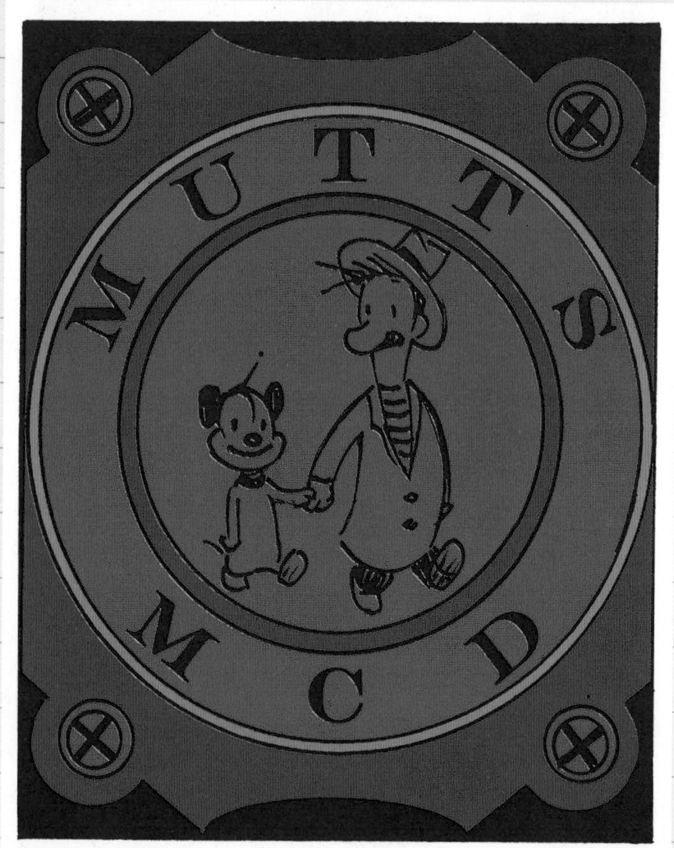
MUTTS
MCD

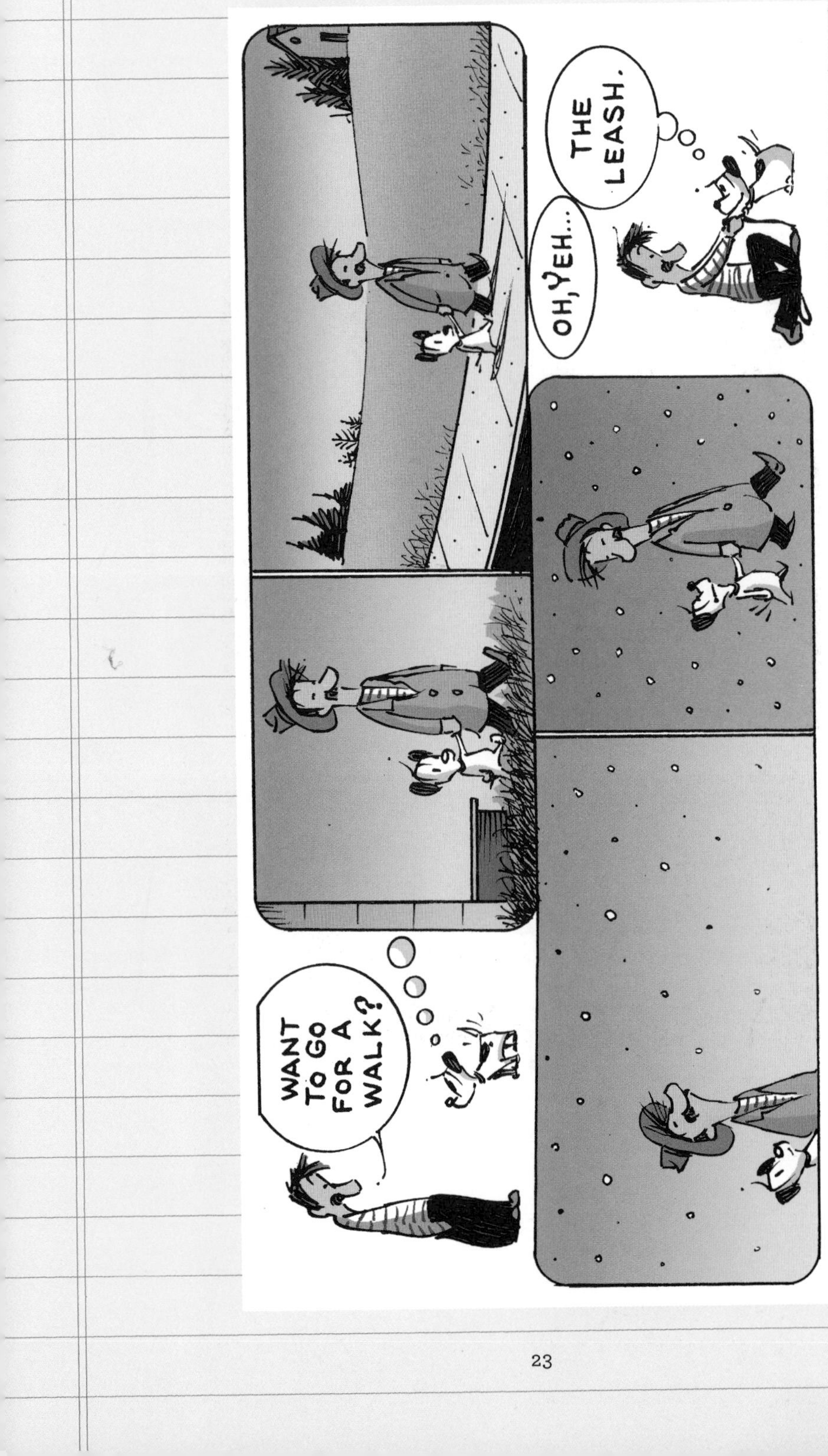
WANT TO GO FOR A WALK?
OH, YEH... THE LEASH.

NOW... NOW... HOLD STILL, EARL.
TA
DA!
WHAT DO YOU THINK?

IT MATCHES MY EYES.

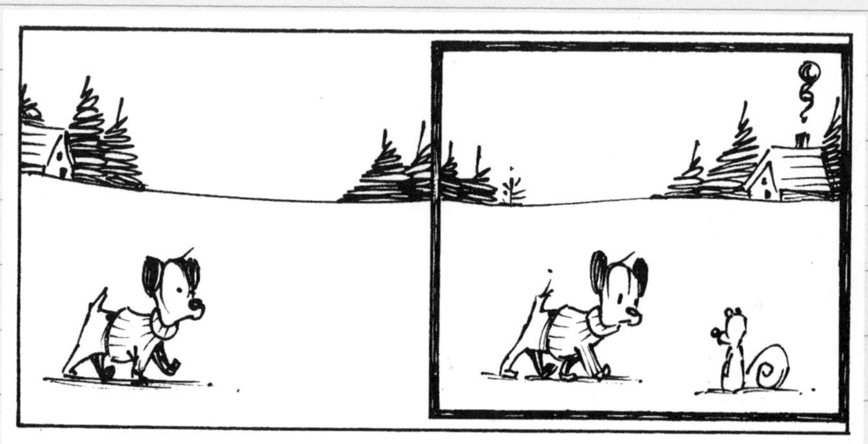

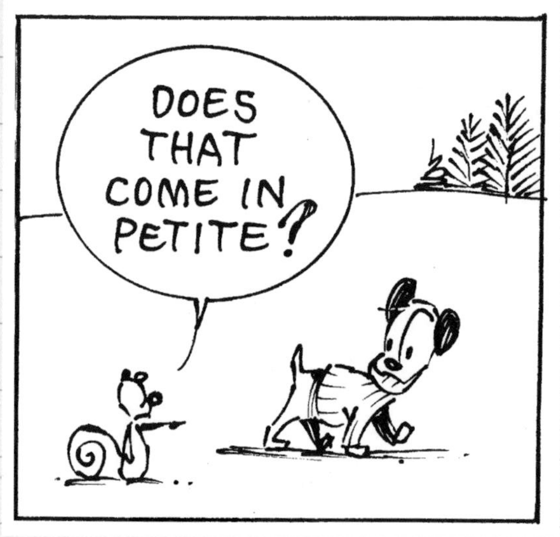
DOES THAT COME IN PETITE?

YOU FORGOT YOUR PIPE.

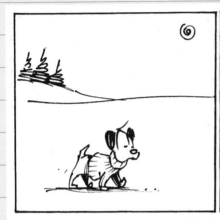

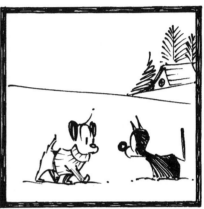

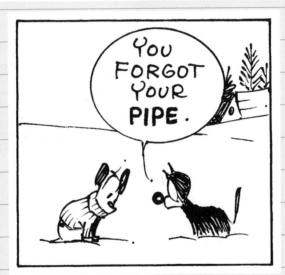

MY GOODNESS!
PUT ON SOME PANTS!

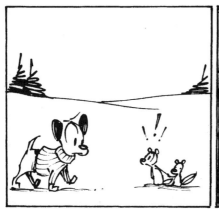

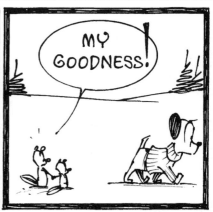

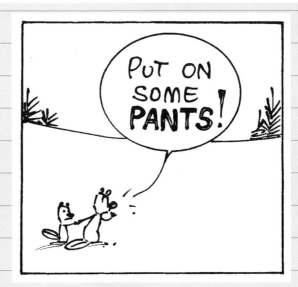

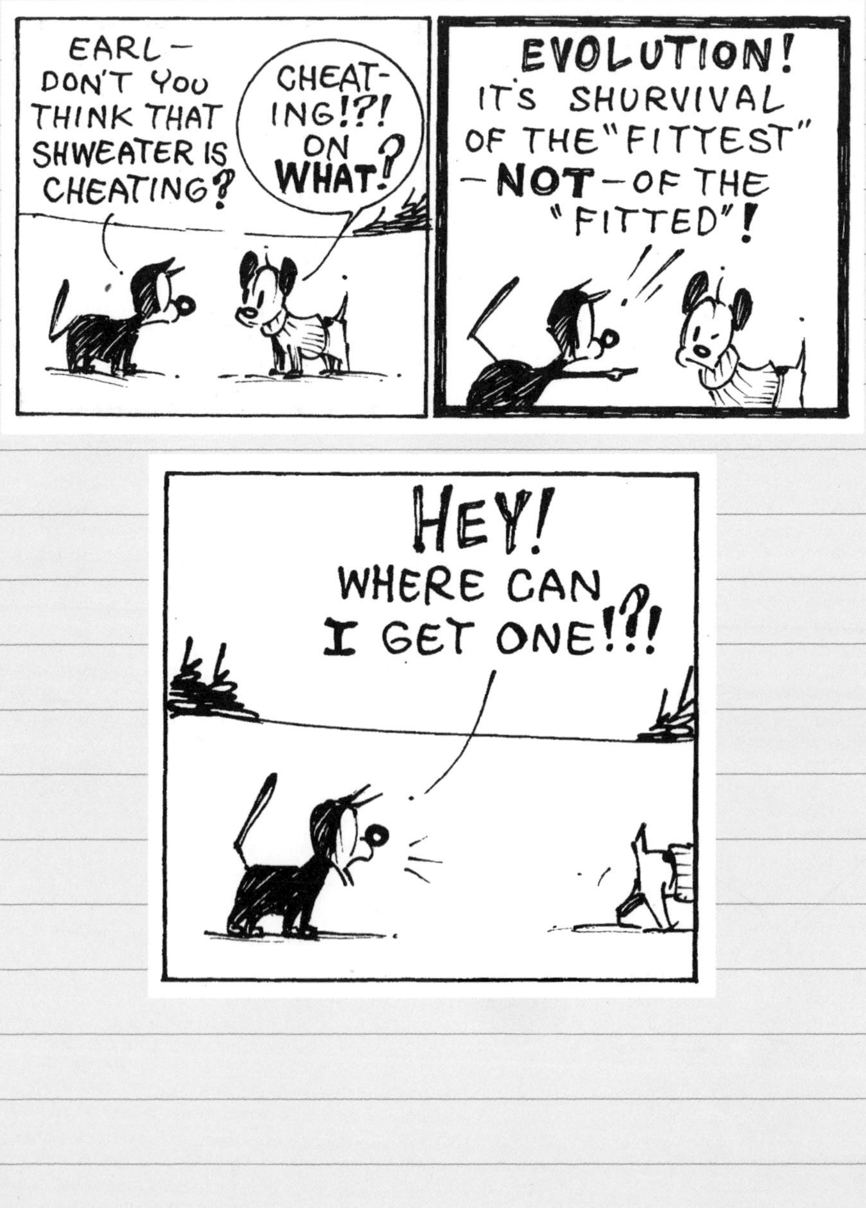
EARL—
DON'T YOU THINK THAT SHWEATER IS CHEATING?
CHEAT-ING!?! ON WHAT!?
EVOLUTION!
IT'S SHURVIVAL OF THE "FITTEST" —NOT— OF THE "FITTED"!
HEY!
WHERE CAN I GET ONE!?!

EARL! HOW COULD YOU LOSE A SWEATER?
SILLY DOG.
LICK LICK LICK

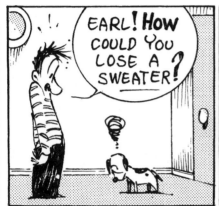

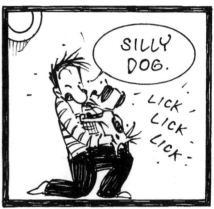

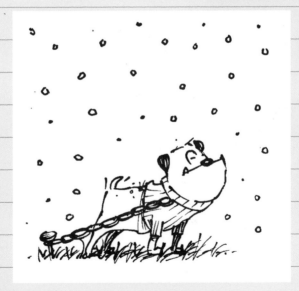

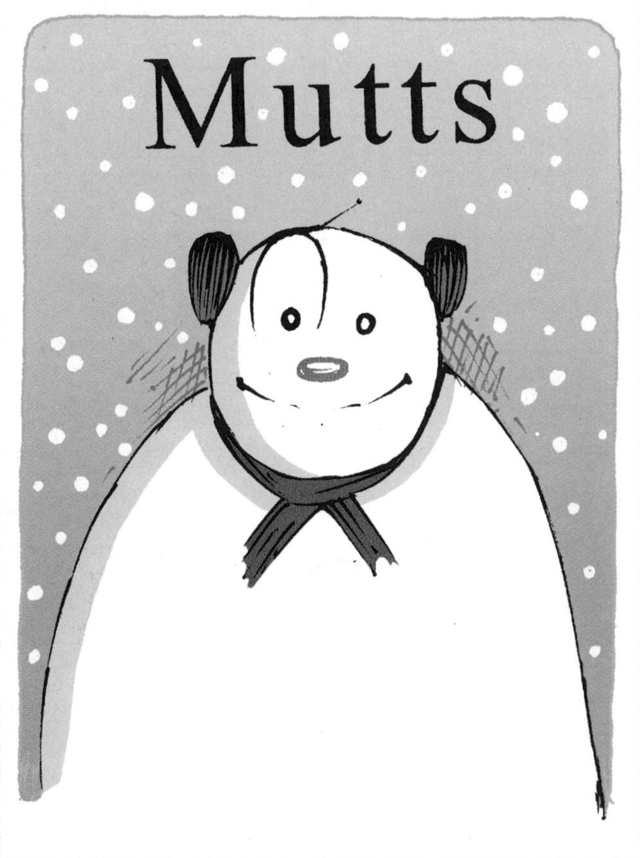
Mutts

!
GEE...
I DIDN'T THINK
CATS WORE HATS.
THAT
WAS LAST
SEASON.

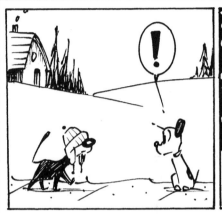

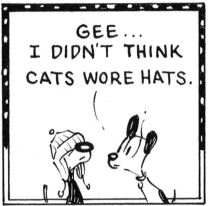

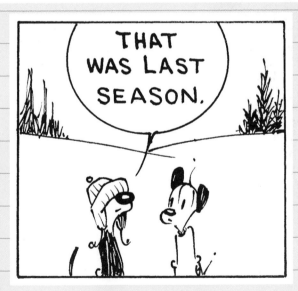

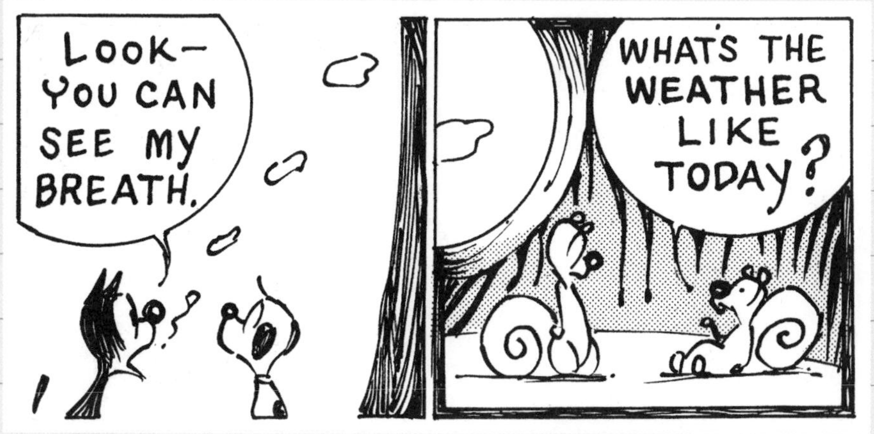
LOOK—
YOU CAN
SEE MY
BREATH.
WHAT'S THE
WEATHER
LIKE
TODAY?

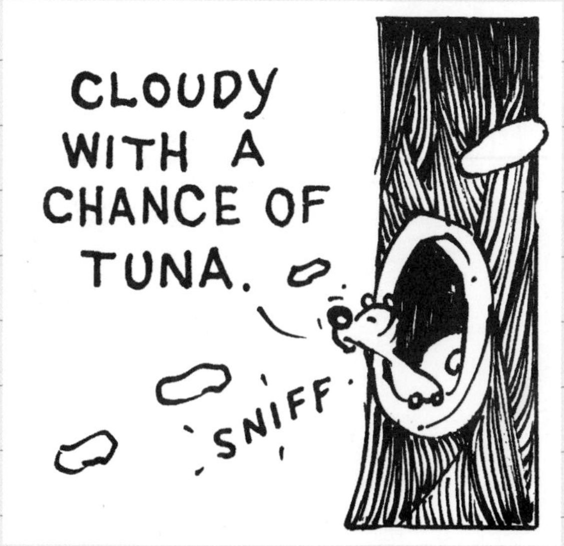
CLOUDY
WITH A
CHANCE OF
TUNA.
SNIFF

BEARS DON'T HIBERNATE IN HOTELS, MOOCH.
THEY STAY IN CAVES!
OH.

HOW'S THE ROOM SHERVICE THERE?

LOOK!
THERE'S A BEAR CAVE!!!
THAT'S WHERE THEY HIBERNATE. LET'S VISIT!
YESH!

MY FIRST SHLEEP-OVER.

THIS IS THE CAVE WHERE THE BEARS HIBERNATE.
SHWEET.

WHERE'S THE THERMO-STAT?

LOOK, MOOCH! THERE'S A HIBERNATING BEAR!!!

BORING.

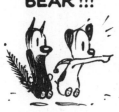

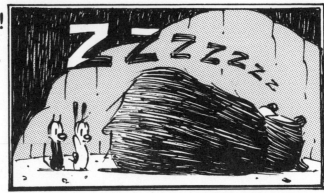

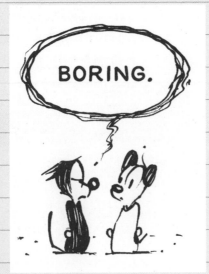

MUTTS

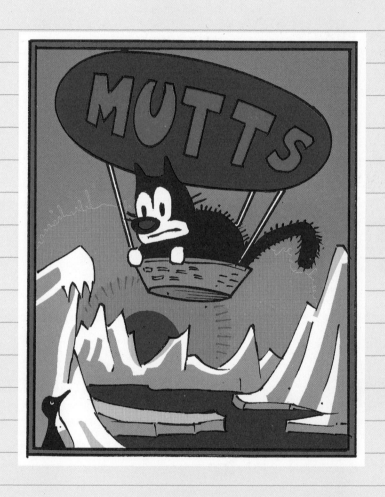

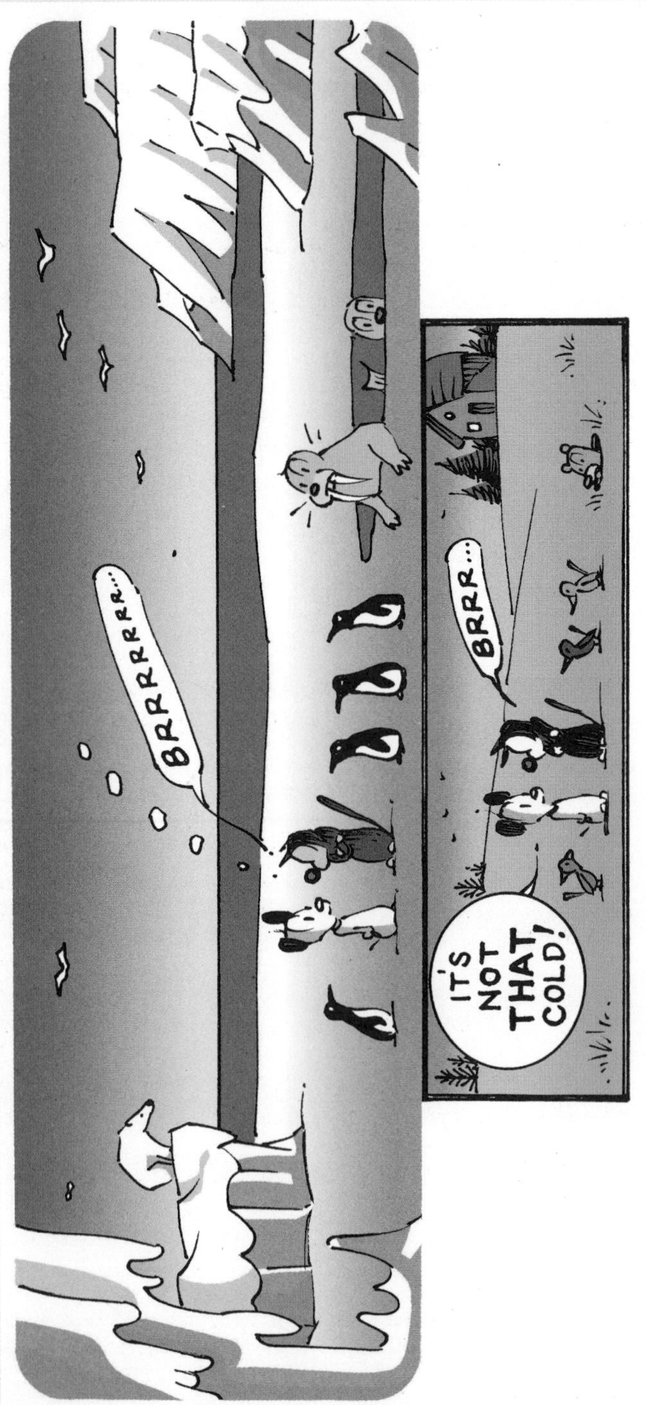
BRRRRRRRR...
BRRR...
IT'S NOT THAT COLD!

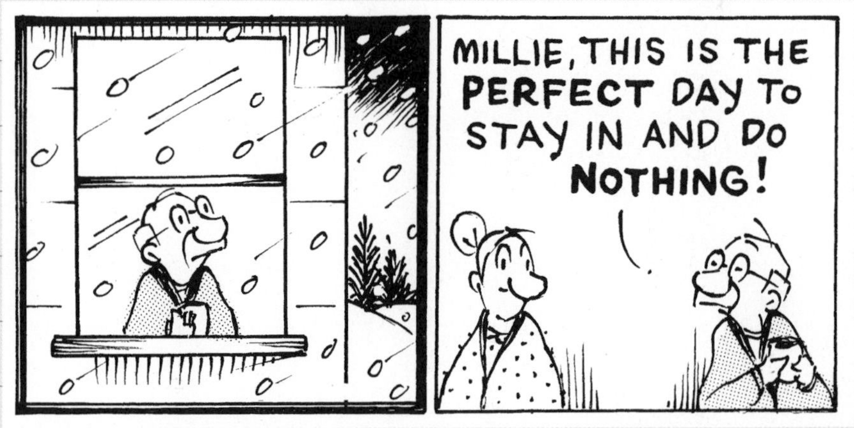
MILLIE, THIS IS THE PERFECT DAY TO STAY IN AND DO NOTHING!

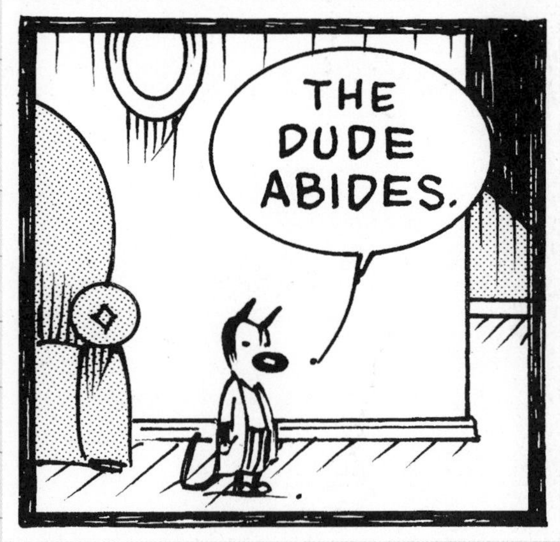
THE DUDE ABIDES.

I'M LOOKING FOR TWO IDENTICAL SHNOWFLAKES
IT MIGHT HELP IF IT WAS SNOW-ING.
HA!
I LIKE A CHALLENGE.

I'M SEARCHING FOR TWO IDENTICAL SHNOWFLAKES.
WHY?
FOR THE BIG PRIZE!
!?!
THERE IS A BIG PRIZE
ISN'T THERE?

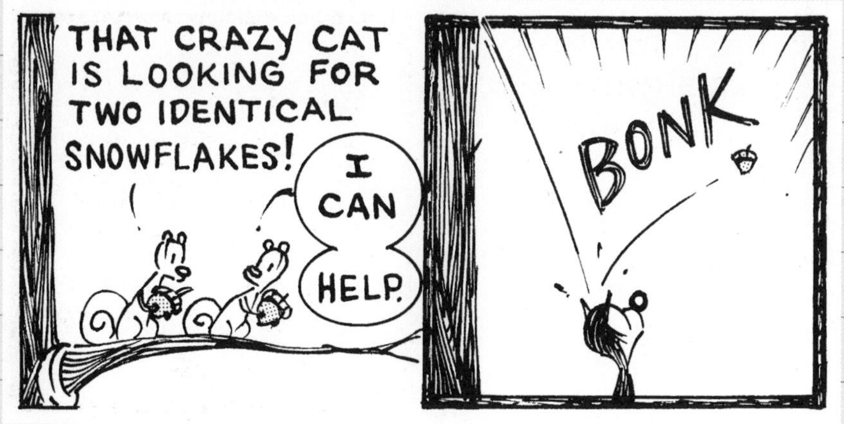
THAT CRAZY CAT IS LOOKING FOR TWO IDENTICAL SNOWFLAKES!
I CAN HELP.
BONK

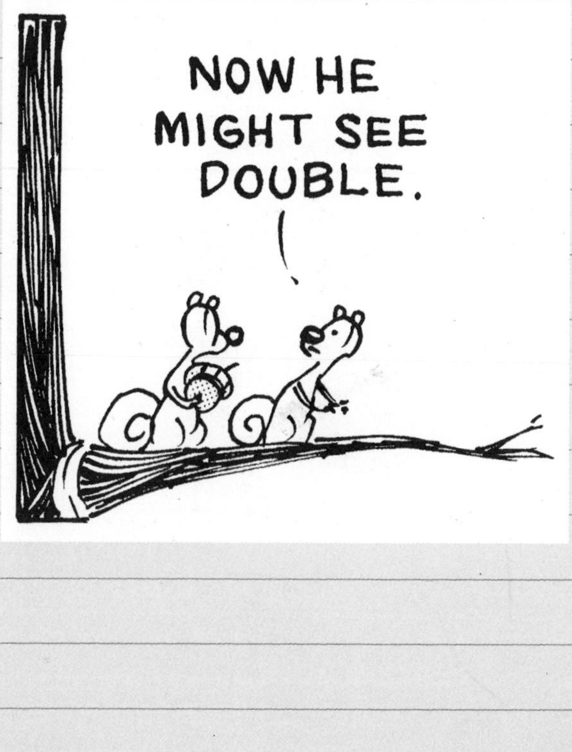
NOW HE MIGHT SEE DOUBLE.

EUREKA!– TWO SHNOWFLAKES THAT SHMIGHT BE IDENTICAL!
WELL?
I DUNNO...
THEY ALL LOOK THE SAME TO ME.

A·HA! TWO PERHAPS IDENTICAL SHNOW-FLAKES!
WHAT DID YOURS LOOK LIKE?

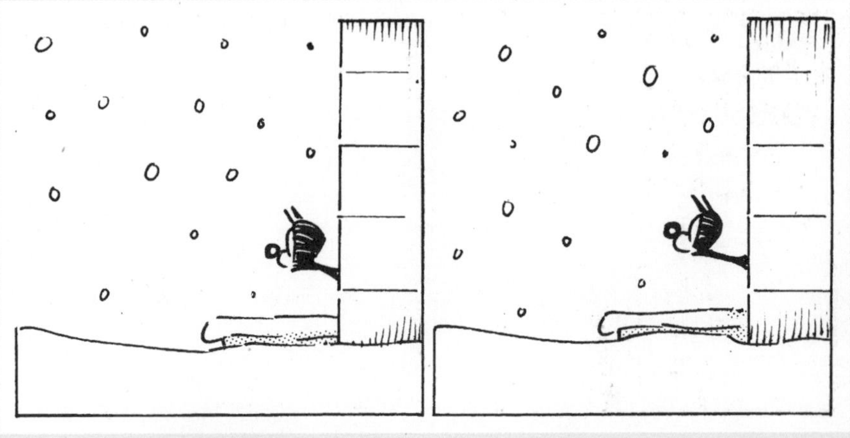

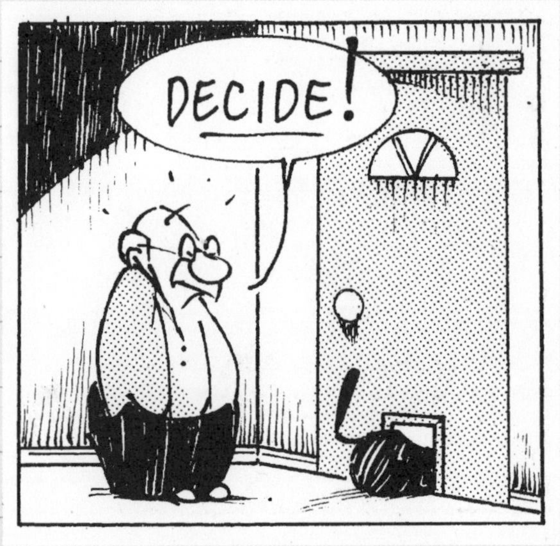
DECIDE!

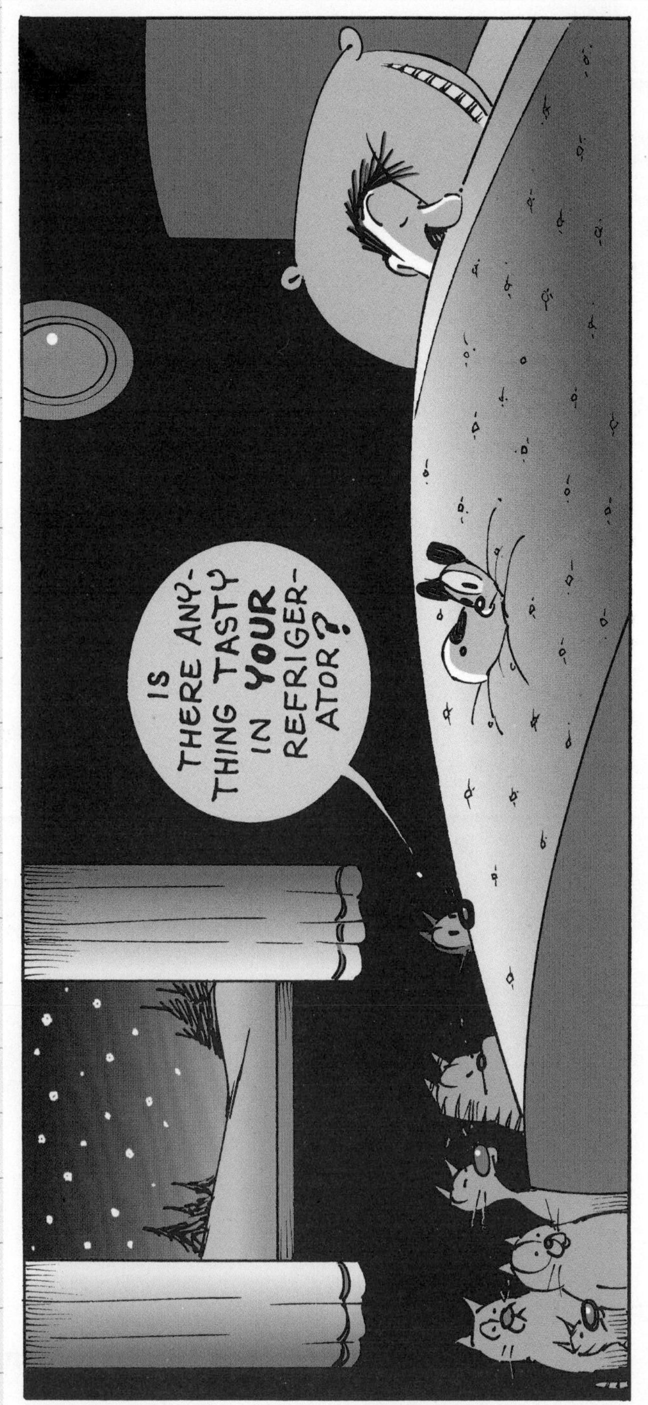
IS THERE ANY-THING TASTY IN **YOUR** REFRIGER-ATOR?

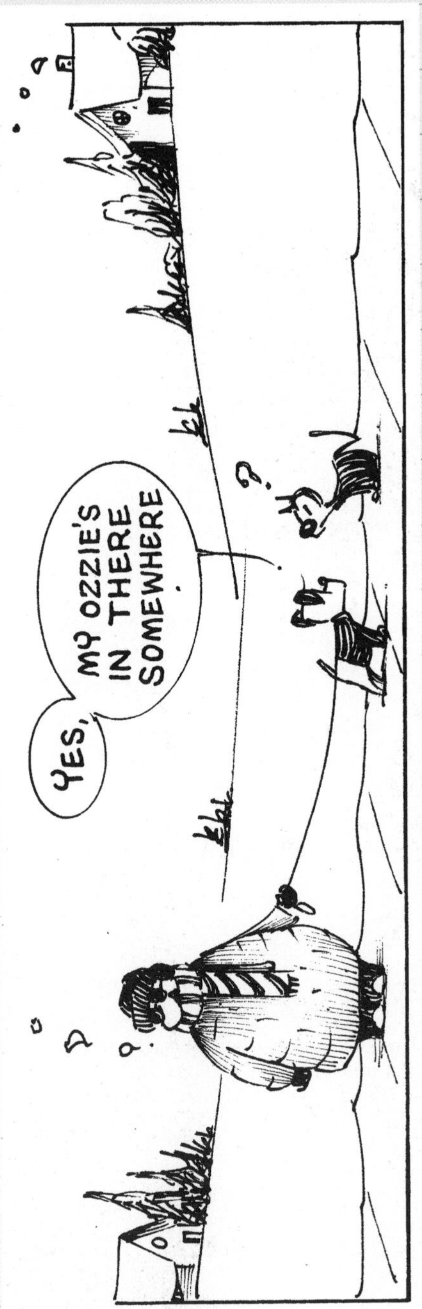
YES,
MY OZZIE'S IN THERE SOMEWHERE

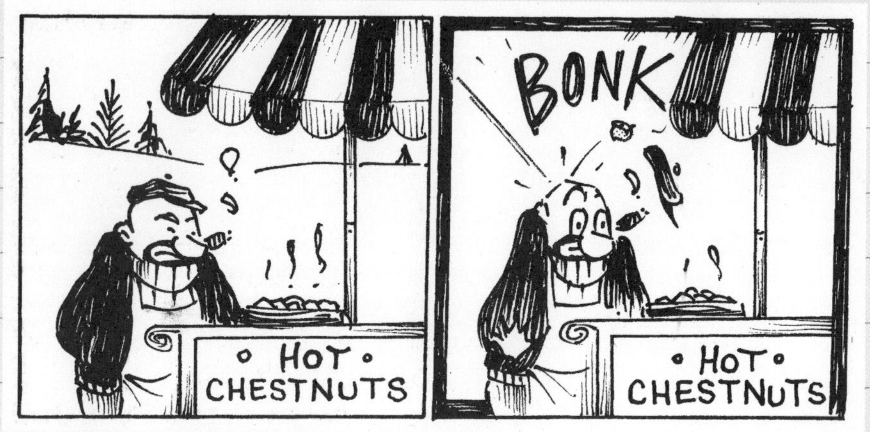
• HOT •
CHESTNUTS
BONK
• HOT •
CHESTNUTS

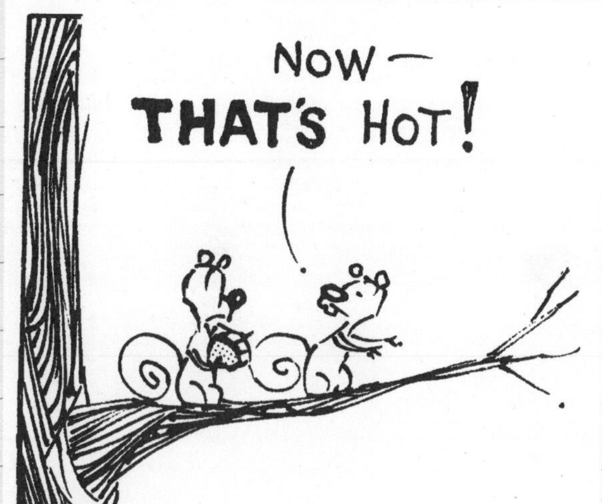
NOW —
THAT'S HOT!

No TWO SNOW-FLAKES ARE ALIKE.
I MUSHT NEED GLASSES.

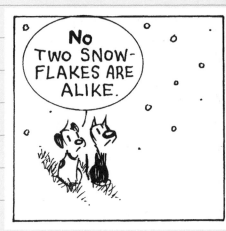

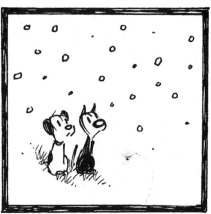

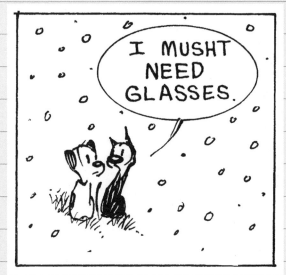

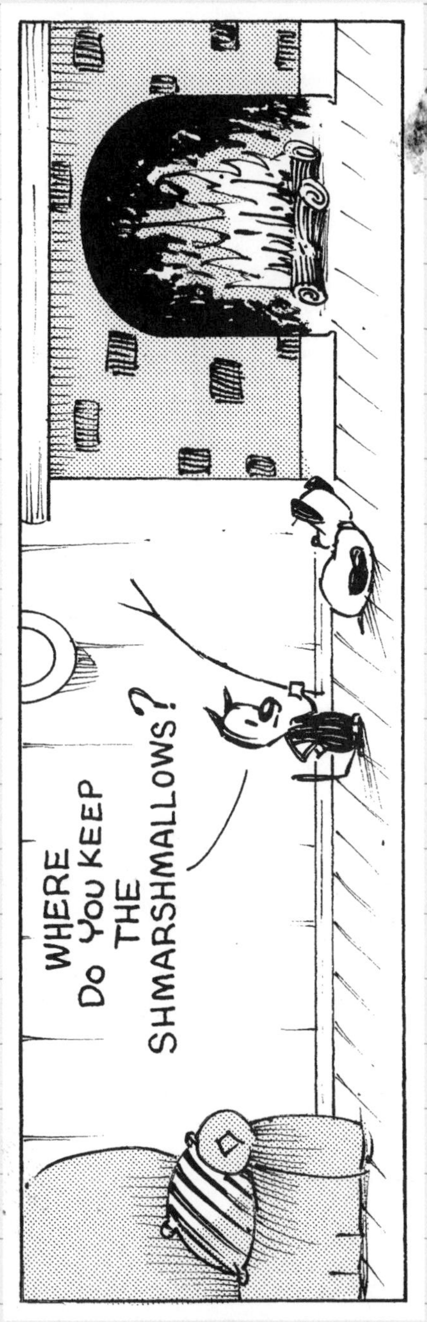
WHERE DO YOU KEEP THE SHMARSHMALLOWS?

OH, WELL...
I'LL SEE YOU IN APRIL.

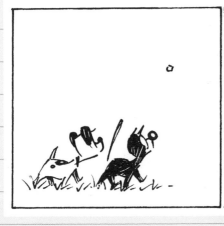

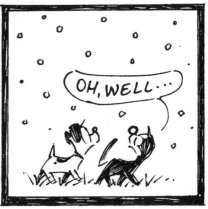

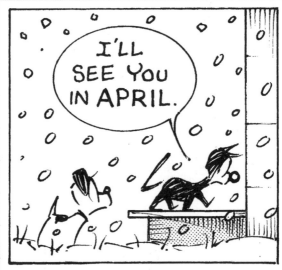

BRRR... I HOPE YOU GUYS ARE WARM ENOUGH IN YOUR LI'L FUR COATS!
SURE...
I HAVE A SHWEATER ON UNDER-NEATH.

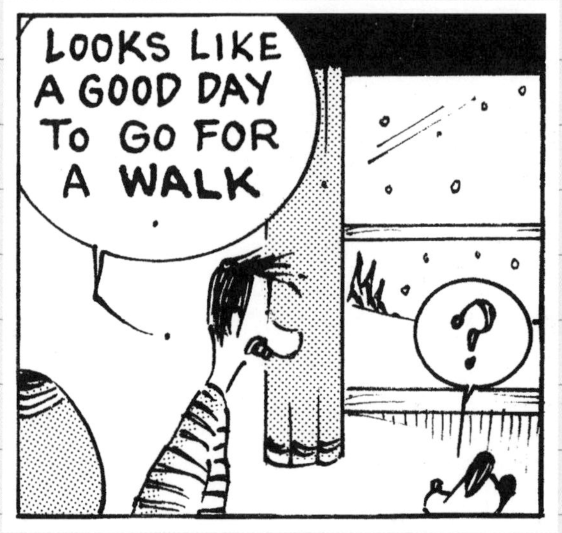
LOOKS LIKE A GOOD DAY TO GO FOR A WALK
?

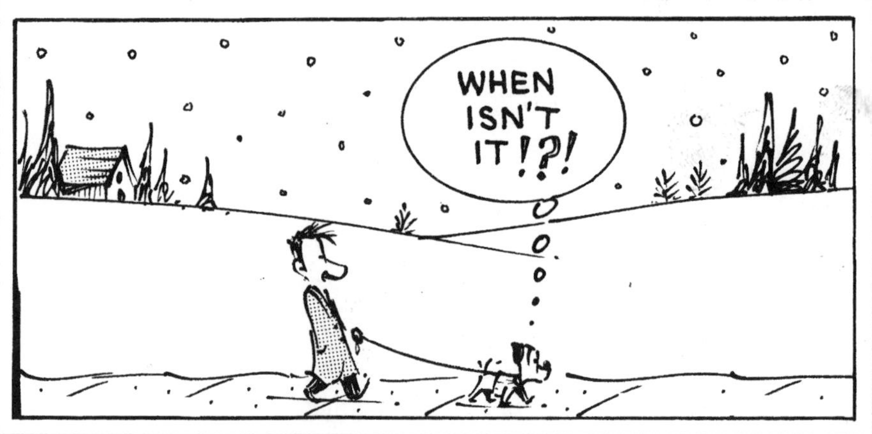
WHEN ISN'T IT!?!

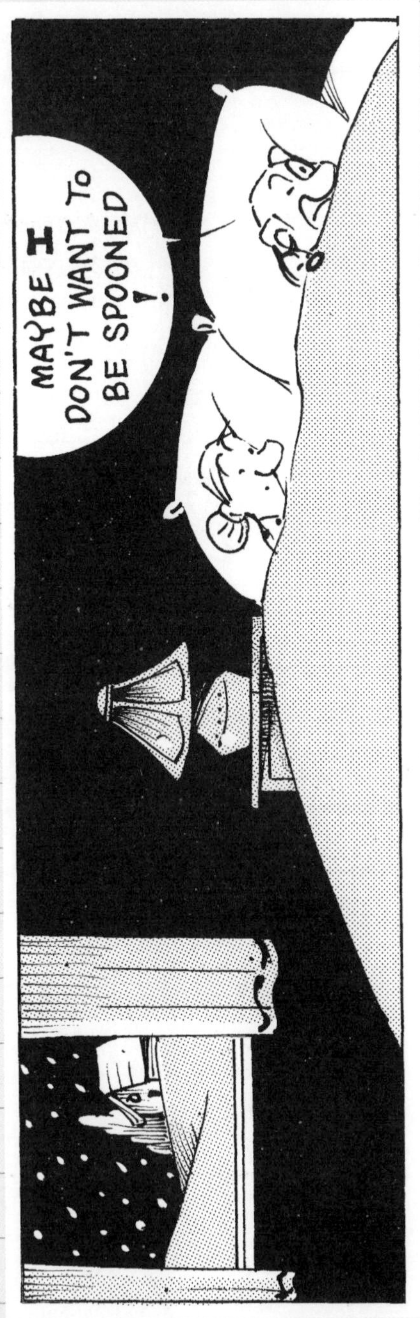
MAYBE I DON'T WANT TO BE SPOONED!

OH, 'SHNIFF', EARL, 'SNIFF' I THINK 'COFF' I HAB A COLD. 'SNIFF'
DO YOU 'SNIFF' THINK 'COFF' IT'S 'SNIFFLE' CATCHY?
I 'SHNIFFLE' 'COUGH' DOUBT IT.
THAT'S 'ACHOO' GOOD.

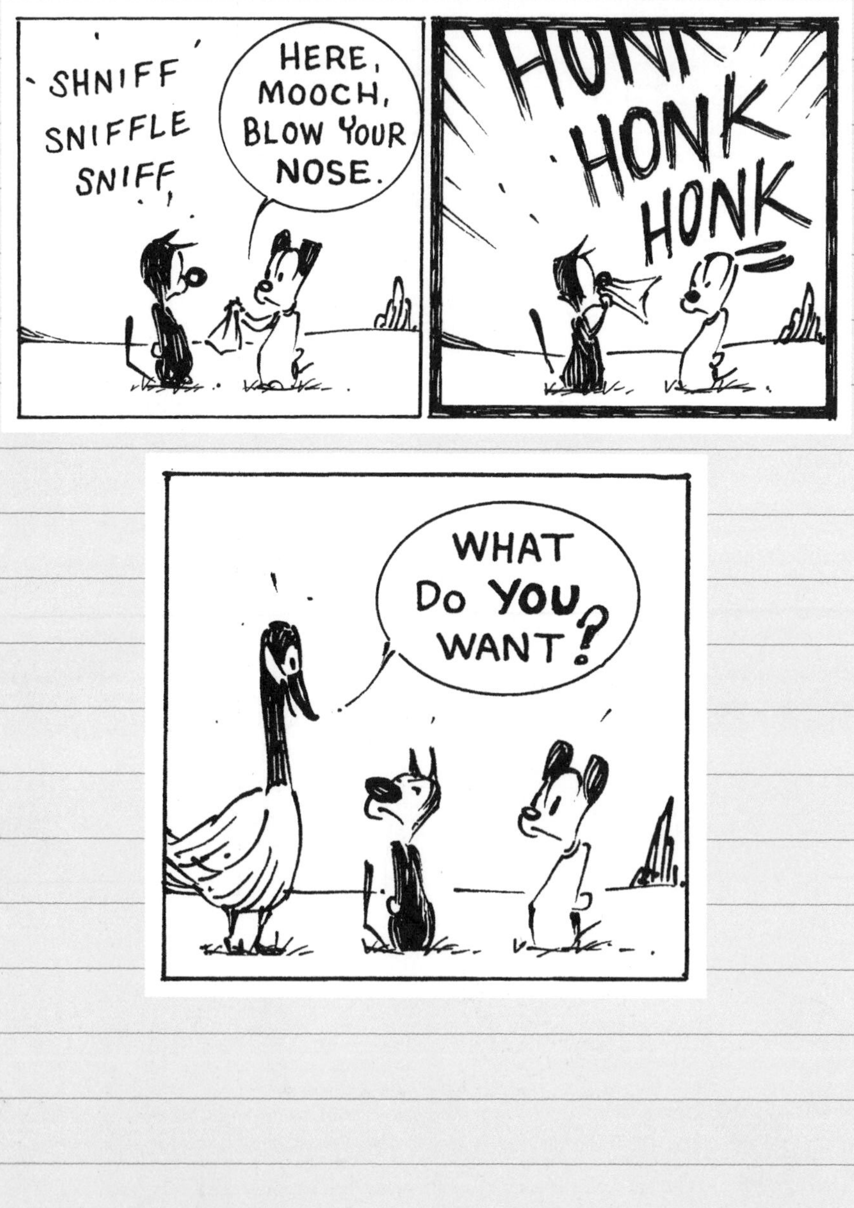
SHNIFF
SNIFFLE
SNIFF
HERE, MOOCH, BLOW YOUR NOSE.
HONK
HONK
WHAT DO YOU WANT?

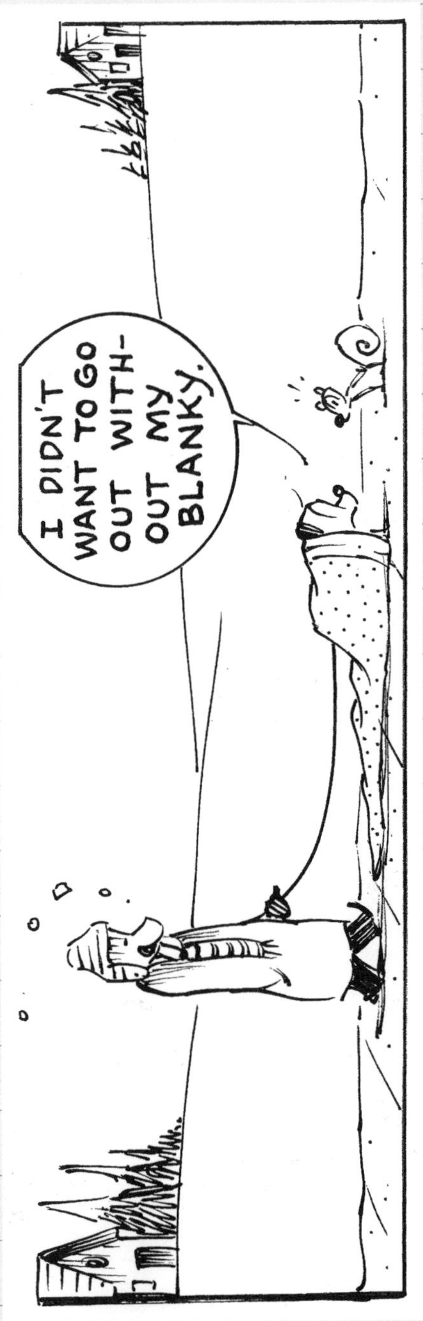
I DIDN'T WANT TO GO OUT WITH-OUT MY BLANKY.

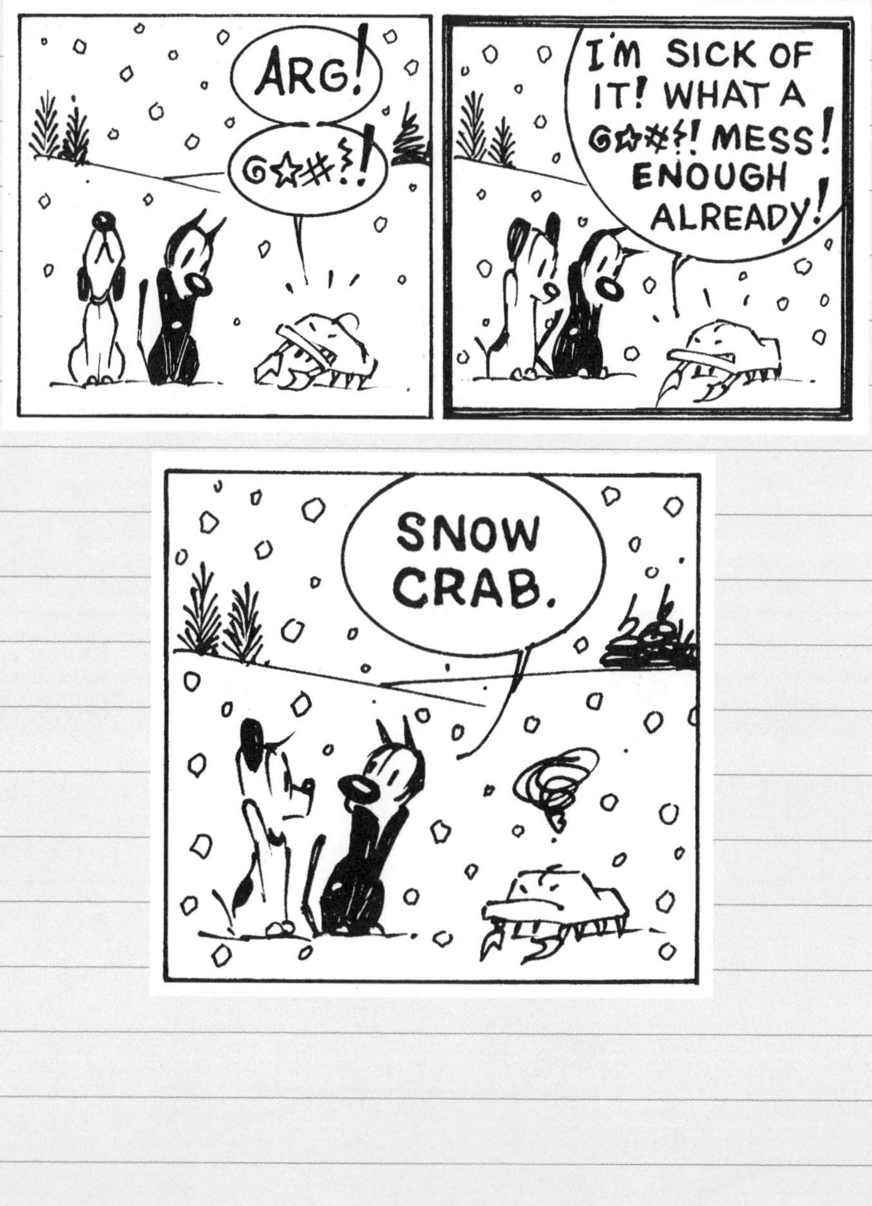
ARG!
G☆#⸮!
I'M SICK OF IT! WHAT A G☆#⸮! MESS! ENOUGH ALREADY!
SNOW CRAB.

YOU'RE STILL IN BED!?!
IT'S A SHNOW DAY.

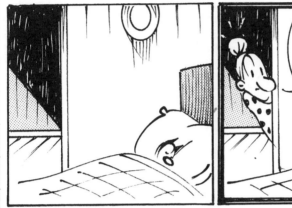

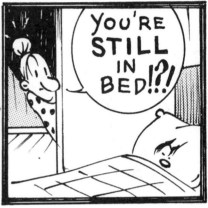

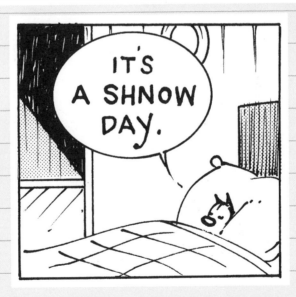

EARL, I LOSHT MY PURR! HOW WILL I KNOW IF I'M HAPPY!?!
JUST WAG YOUR TAIL, MOOCHIE!
HA!
HE DOESN'T DO A THING I SHAY!!!

I'LL FIND YOUR LOST PURR, MOOCH! GIVE ME ITS SCENT, AND MY KEEN SENSE OF SMELL WILL TRACK IT DOWN!
SHNIFF
SHNIFF
SNIFF
QUICK!
–TO THE DUMPSTER BEHIND THE FISH MARKET!

WHERE ARE YOU GOING, MOOCH!?!
I'M OFF TO FIND MY PURR, EARL!
WHAT'S IN THE BAG?
YOUR LUNCH.

SO YOU'RE TRYING TO FIND YOUR LOST PURR, MOOCH...
HA! GOOD LUCK!
I HAVEN'T BEEN IN TOUCH WITH MY PURR IN YEARS!
DO YOU MISSH IT?
HECK NO! WHO COULD SLEEP WITH ALL THAT RACKET!?!

WHAT'S A KITTY WITHOUT HIS **PURR!?!** I'LL SEARCH THE GLOBE TO FIND MINE!
OOF...
I HOPE IT'S SHOMEWHERE WARM.

SHTINKY! WHAT ARE YOU DOING OUT HERE?
THE USUAL. I'M LOST...
YESH. I UNDER-SHTAND. I'M OUT TRYING TO FIND MY "PURR".
...BUT NOT **THAT** LOST.

I LOST MY PURR, SHTINKY.
I KNOW WHERE IT IS, MOOCH.
YOU DO!?!
SURE! IT'S THAT FEELING OF JOY DEEP INSIDE YOU.

I THOUGHT THAT WAS THE EGGSHNOG.

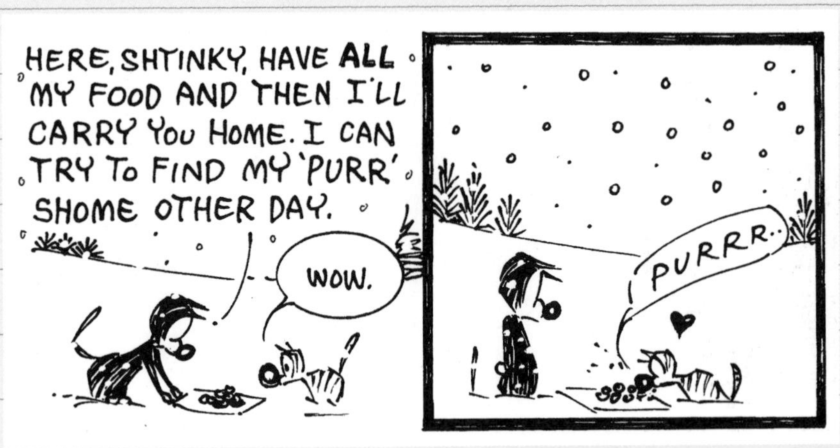
HERE, SHTINKY, HAVE ALL MY FOOD AND THEN I'LL CARRY YOU HOME. I CAN TRY TO FIND MY 'PURR' SHOME OTHER DAY.
WOW.
PURRR..

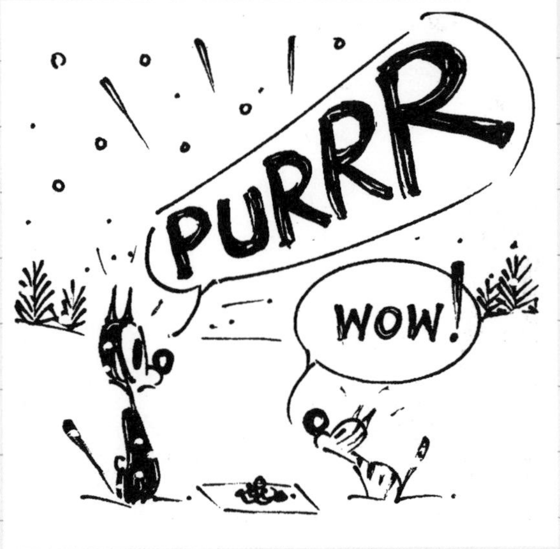
PURRR
WOW!

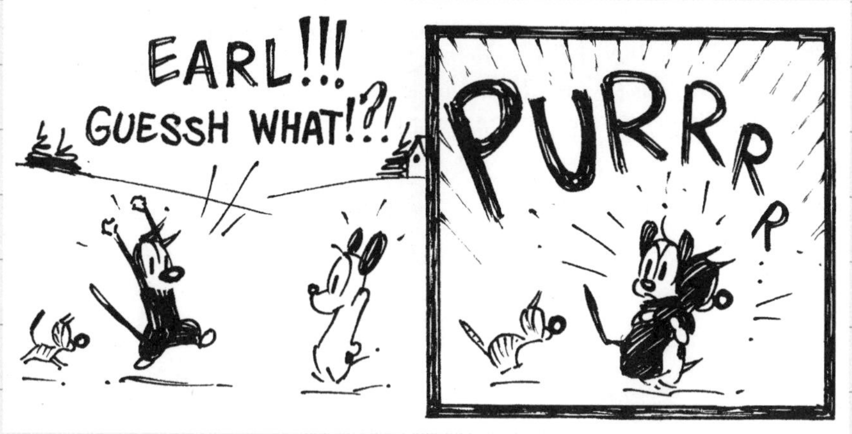
EARL!!!
GUESSH WHAT!?!
PURRRR

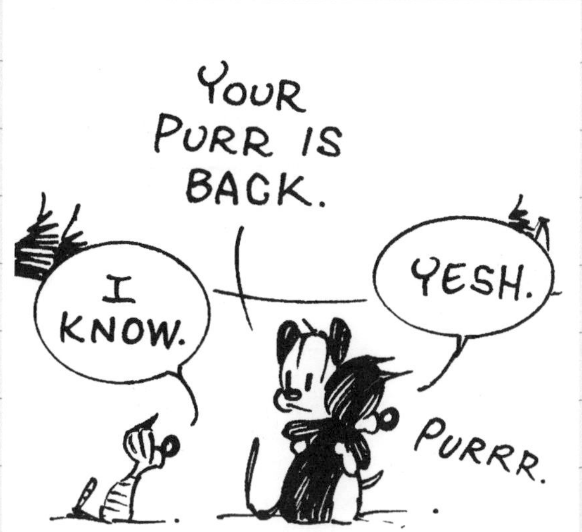
YOUR PURR IS BACK.
I KNOW.
YESH.
PURRR.

BONK
BONK
NICE DAY FOR A WALK.

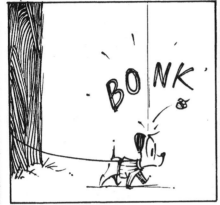

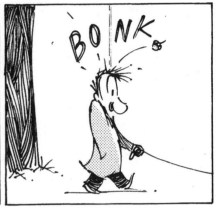

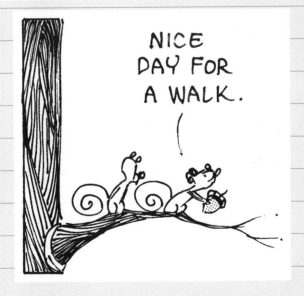

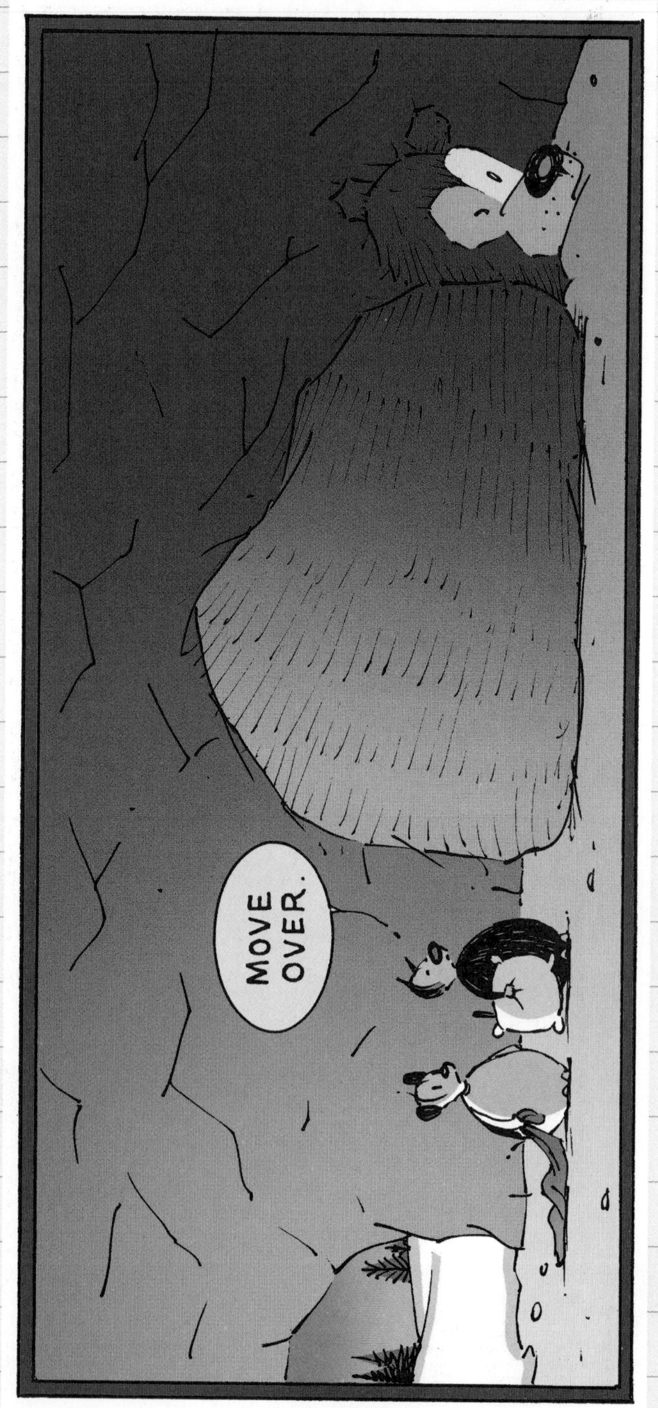
MOVE OVER.

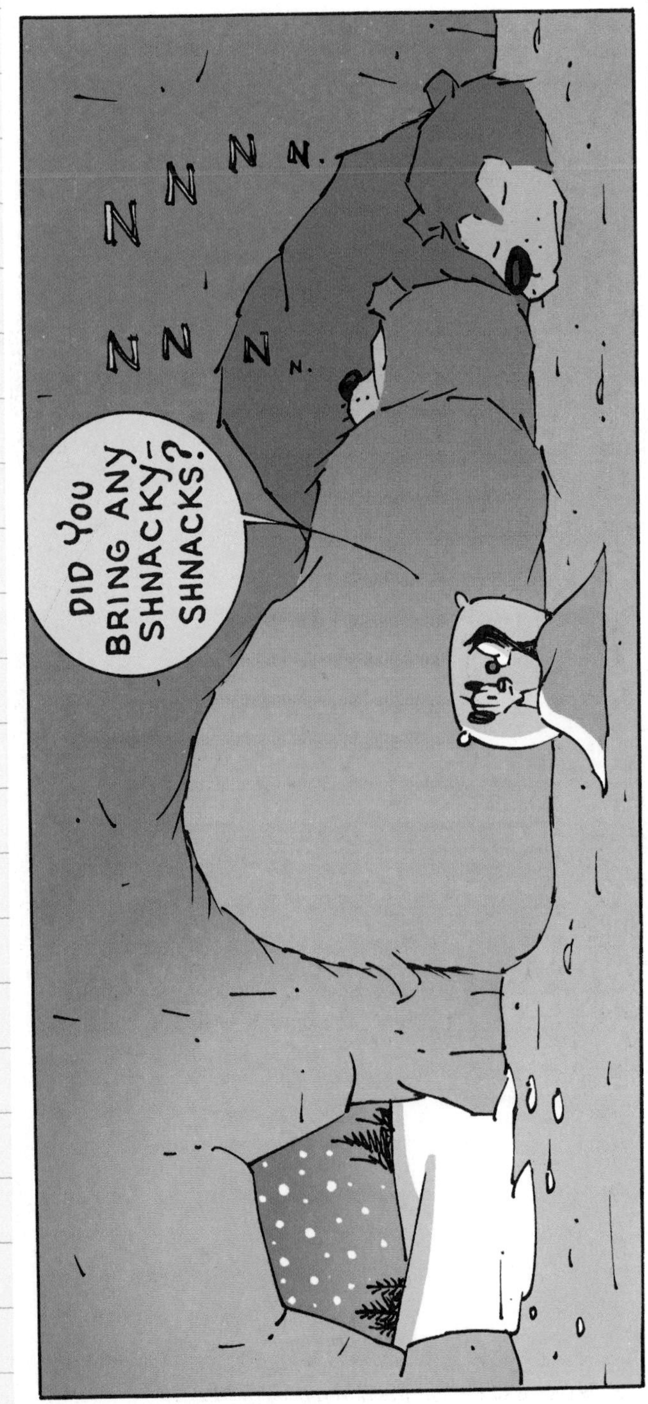
ZZZz.
ZZZz.
DID YOU BRING ANY SHNACKY-SHNACKS?

Z.Z.Z.Z...
EARL
EARL!
WAKE UP!
WHA...

IT'S TIME TO HIBERNATE!

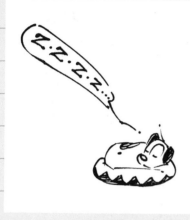

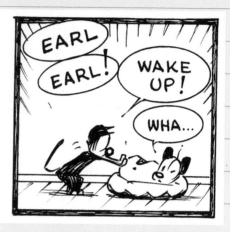

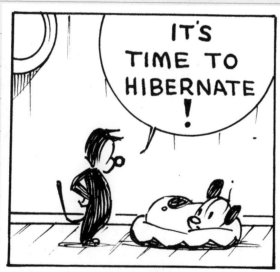

IT'S HIBERNATING TIME!
TIME TO PUT ON SHOME EXTRA BODY FAT FOR A LONG WINTER'S NAP.
CHOMP
CHOMP
OH, TOMMY, MY LI'L CHUMMY. THERE... THERE...
PAT
PAT
THAT SHOULD GET ME THRU THE NEXT TWO HOURS.

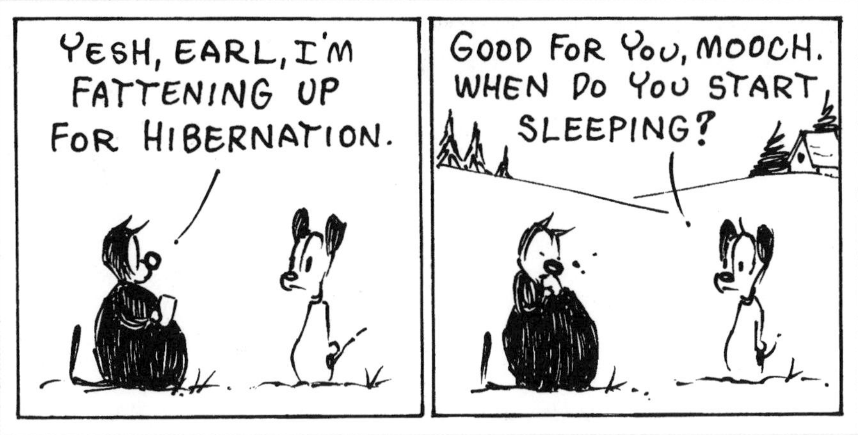
YESH, EARL, I'M FATTENING UP FOR HIBERNATION.
GOOD FOR YOU, MOOCH. WHEN DO YOU START SLEEPING?

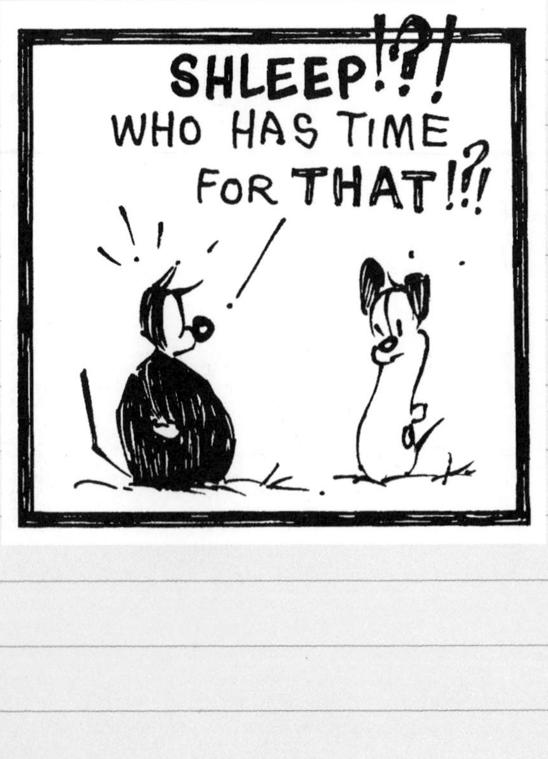
SHLEEP!?! WHO HAS TIME FOR THAT!?!

AUGH! ooOOH MY POOR PO' TUMMY! WATTA ACHE!!!
MOOCH— COULD IT BE SOMETHING YOU ATE?
DO YOU THINK!?!

SO, MOOCH, THE PLAN IS TO **FATTEN** UP AND HIBERNATE IN **BED** FOR THE REST OF THE WINTER!
YESH.
UMF.
OOF.
ARG.
WHAT'S PLAN **B**?
FOO.

WE FATTENED UP SO MUCH TO HIBERNATE WE CAN'T MAKE IT UP ON THE BED!
YESH.
WHAT ARE WE GOING TO DO!?!
LET'S EAT!
WE'RE GOING TO NEED OUR SHTRENGTH.

I THINK I'LL SHTAY IN BED ALL DAY TODAY.
mmmmm...
A MAN WITH A PLAN.

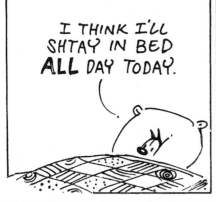

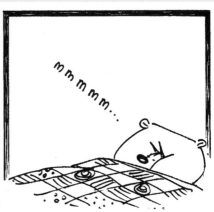

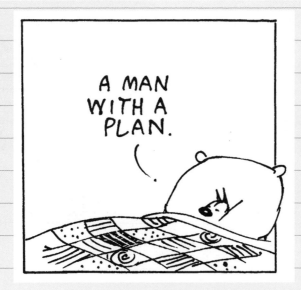

MOOCH! ARE YOU GOING TO STAY IN BED ALL WINTER!?!
I'M THINKING ABOUT IT.
THAT'S CRAZY! GET YOUR TUSHIE OUT OF THAT BED RIGHT NOW!
I CAN'T...
HE'S ASHLEEP.

EARL-I'VE DECIDED TO HIBERNATE!
COULD YOU SET THE ALARM FOR APRIL?

MOOCH—
WHAT'S THE FIRST STEP FOR HIBERNATING ALL WINTER?
FINDING A COMFY POSITION.

THIS IS IT! I'M GOING TO HIBERNATE ALL WINTER!
GOOD LUCK.
THANKS
WAKE ME IF ANYTHING HAPPENS!

MOOCH– YOU'RE CRAZY TO STAY IN BED ALL WINTER!!!
YESH...
...AND TOASHTY.
MOVE OVER.

YOU'RE RIGHT, MOOCH— WINTER'S **TOO** LONG. WE'LL HIBERNATE AND IT WILL JUST WOOSH BY!
YESH.
I DON'T HEAR ANY WOOSHING YET.

GOOD NIGHT, MOOCH—
I'LL SEE YOU IN
MY DREAMS.
YESH.

HOW
DO I
GET
THERE?

EARL, HOW WILL WE KNOW WHEN TO SHTOP HIBERNATING?
OUR BODYCLOCKS WILL TELL US.
WHERE'S MY SHNOOZE BUTTON?

MOOCH— MUST YOU SLEEP WITH THAT LI'L PINK SOCK?
SHMIGHT COME IN HANDY.
Z

SHNIFF
SNIFFLE
SNIFF
WHEEZE
SNORT
ACK
FOO
SHNIFF
HONK
SHNIFFY
SHNORT
CHOO
KOFF
HEY!
DON'T GET ME SICK!

EARL, I LOVE HIBERNATING!
LOVE IT!?! YOU HAVEN'T SLEPT A WINK YET!!!
I DON'T LOVE THAT PART.

MOOCHIE!
NATURE CALLED.

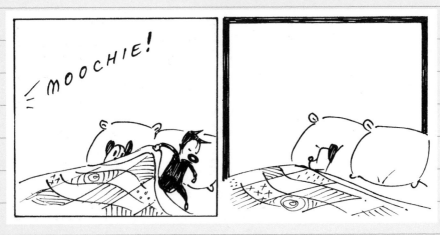

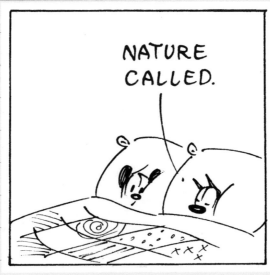

MOOCH, THIS WINTER WE'LL HIBERNATE— LIVING OFF OUR BODY FAT.
SO, I'LL BE EATING AND SHLEEPING AT THE SAME TIME?
YUP.
CAT HEAVEN.

EARL, I BROUGHT IN AN EXSHPERT To TEACH US HOW To HIBERNATE.
MOVE OVER.
WOW! LOOK AT HIM GO!
Z Z Z

I DON'T THINK I CAN HIBERNATE, EARL.
WHAT'S THE MATTER **NOW**, MOOCH!?!
MY JAMMIES ARE **TOO** SHMALL.

MOOCH
WHAT ARE YOU DOING?
SHLEEP-WALK-ING.
WHAT!?! THEN HOW CAN YOU ANSWER ME!?!

SHLEEP-TALKING.

MOOCH, WHY DO YOU THINK YOU'RE 'SHLEEPWALKING'?
BECAUSE
I'M TOO TIRED TO JOG.

ALL THIS SHLEEPWALKING IS GETTING ME TIRED.

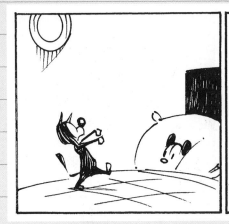

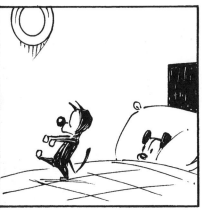

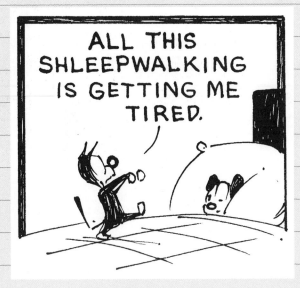

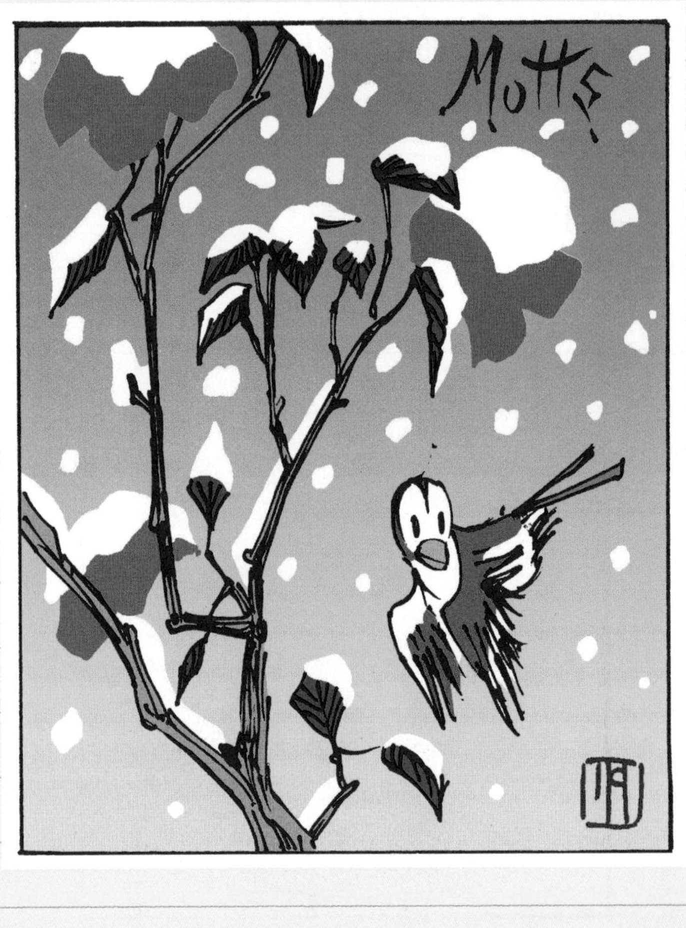
Mutts

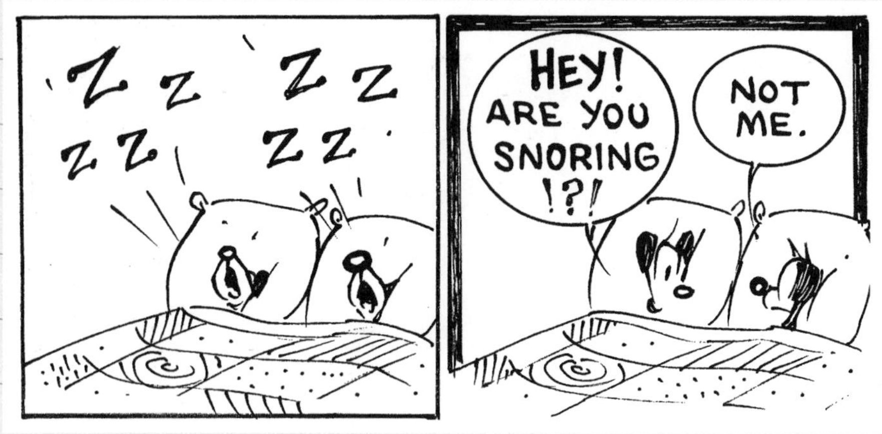
Z Z Z Z Z Z Z Z
HEY! ARE YOU SNORING !?!
NOT ME.

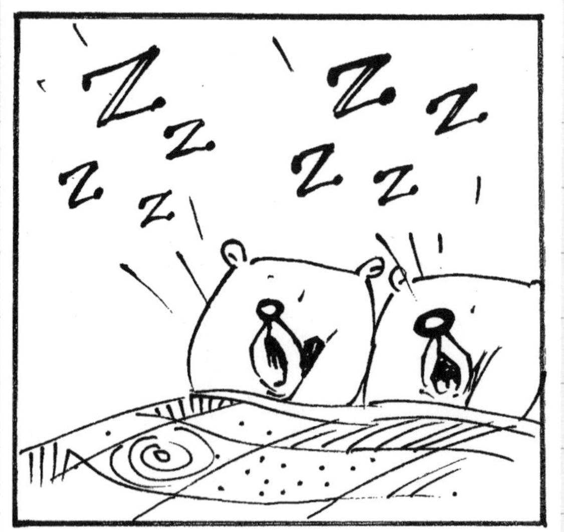
Z Z Z Z Z Z Z Z

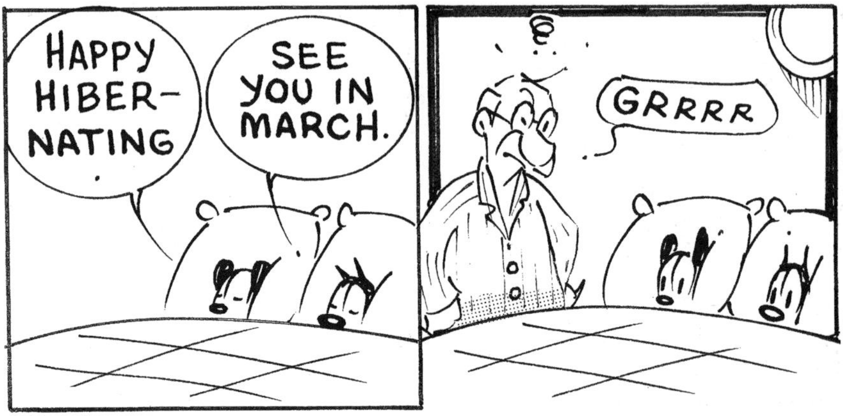
HAPPY HIBER- NATING.
SEE YOU IN MARCH.
GRRRRR

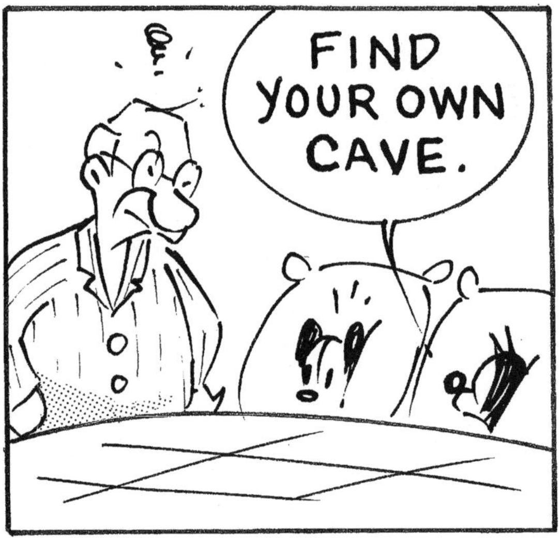
FIND YOUR OWN CAVE.

YOU'RE DONE HIBER-NATING ALREADY!?!
I GUESSH. WHAT TIME IS IT?
FOUR P.M.
WHAT MONTH ?

MOOCH, WHY CAN'T YOU HIBERNATE ?
SHOME-THING'S MISSING

PURRR
Z·Z·Z·Z·Z

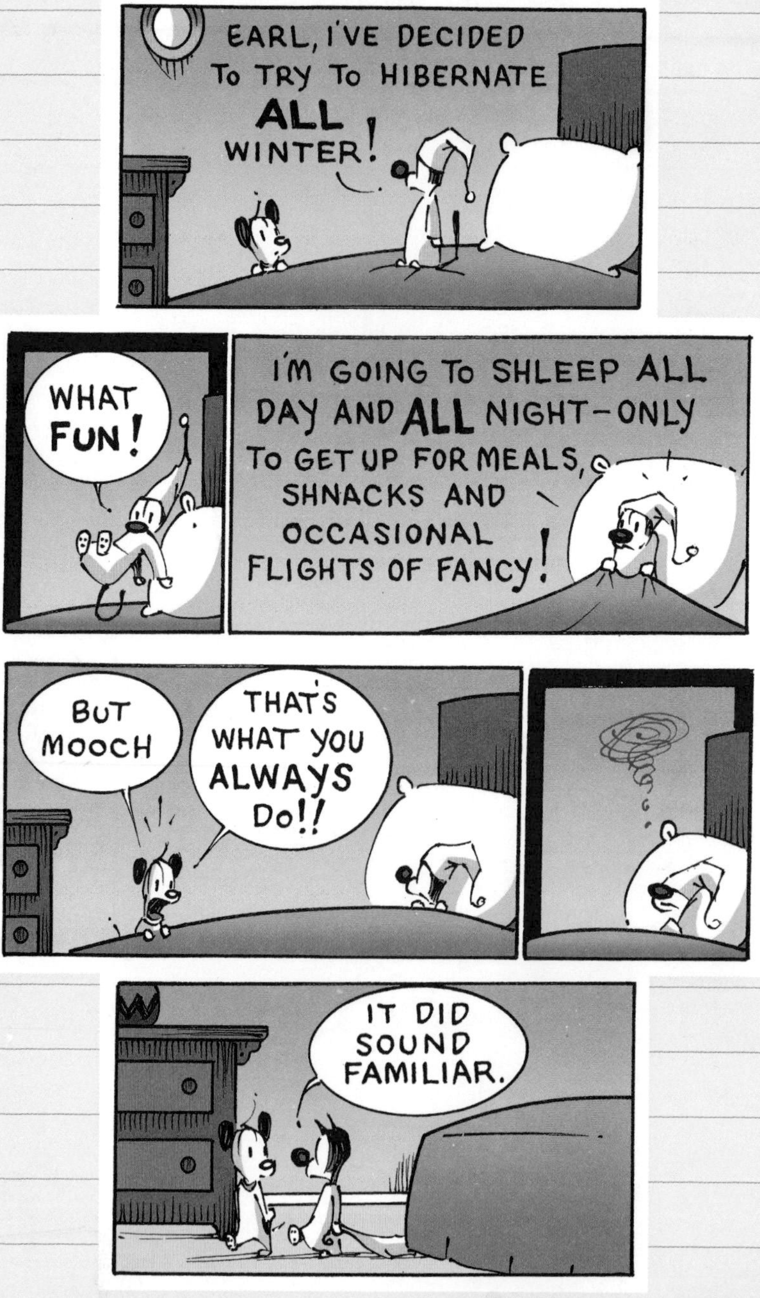

EARL, I'VE DECIDED TO TRY TO HIBERNATE ALL WINTER!
WHAT FUN!
I'M GOING TO SHLEEP ALL DAY AND ALL NIGHT-ONLY TO GET UP FOR MEALS, SHNACKS AND OCCASIONAL FLIGHTS OF FANCY!
BUT MOOCH
THAT'S WHAT YOU ALWAYS DO!!
IT DID SOUND FAMILIAR.

MUTTS **W**ORLD

DRAWN BY P.L.McDONNELL

WE'RE LITTLE SNOW-FLAKES
FROM HEAVEN
WE ARE ALL UNIQUE
JUST LIKE YOU
WE'RE HERE ON EARTH
TO BECOME ONE.
IT'S DEEP.
YESH.

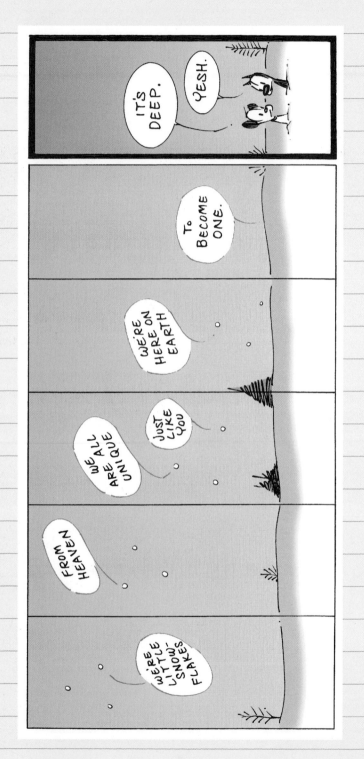

LET'S HEAR IT FOR THE CAT!

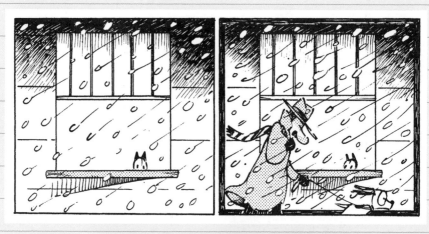

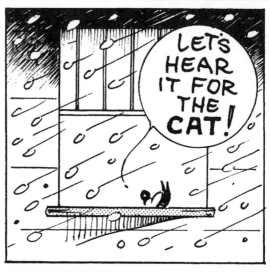

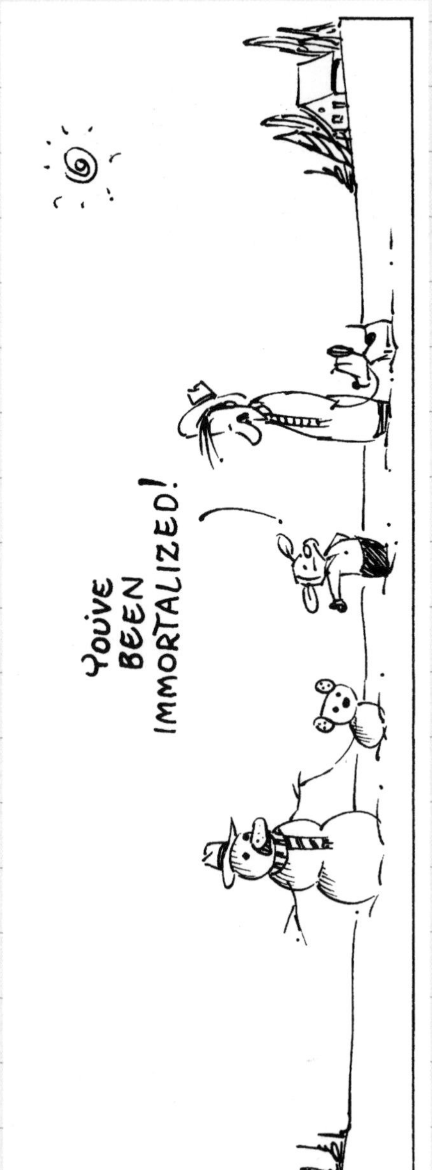
YOU'VE BEEN IMMORTALIZED!

MUSH!
MUSH!
SHWEET TALK WILL GET YOU NOWHERE!

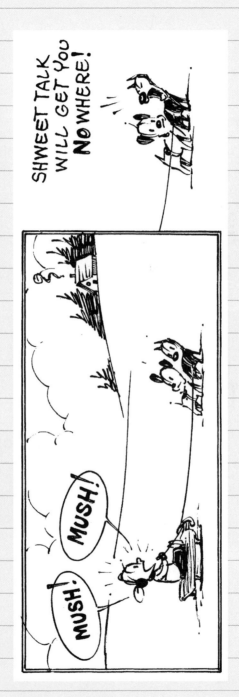

BRRRR, IT LOOKS LIKE A BLIZZARD!
DON'T WORRY, MILLIE, WE'RE PREPARED FOR ANYTHING

LITTLE PINK THERMAL SOCK
LITTLE PINK THERMAL SOCK

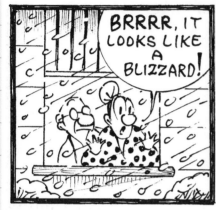

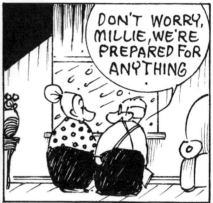

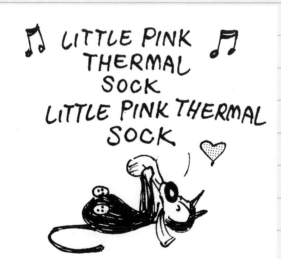

NO TWO SNOWFLAKES ARE ALIKE.
WHO KEEPS THESE RECORDS!?!

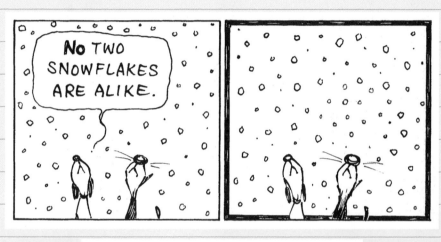

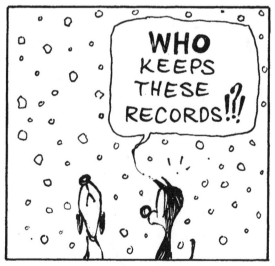

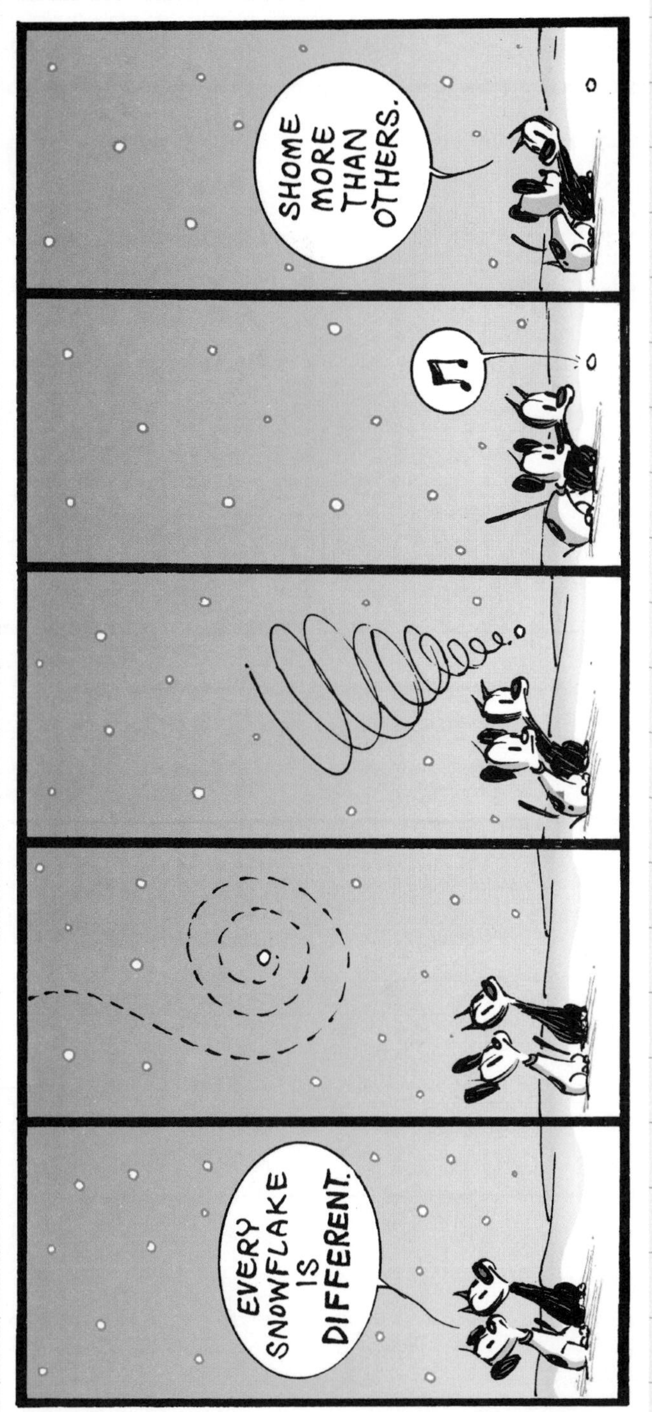
EVERY SNOWFLAKE IS DIFFERENT.
SHOME MORE THAN OTHERS.

BRRRR...
I FORGOT MY MITTEN!
YOU MEAN MITTENS!
WHAT DID YOU SAY?

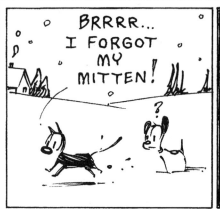

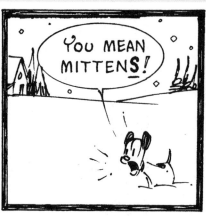

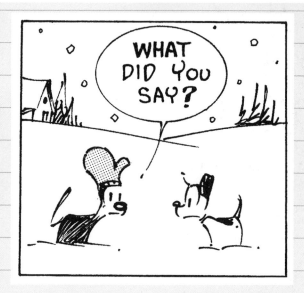

EARL, LOOK AT WHAT'S IN MY BACK-YARD!
I ALWAYS WANTED A PONY.

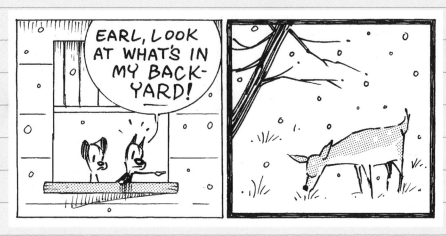

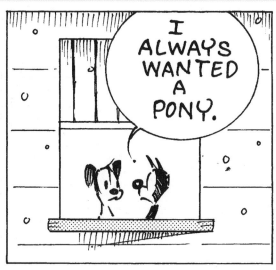

LOOK, EARL! MILLIE GOT ME A PONY FOR CHRIST-MAS!
THAT'S A DEER!
YESH! THAT WOMAN'S A REAL SHWEETIE!

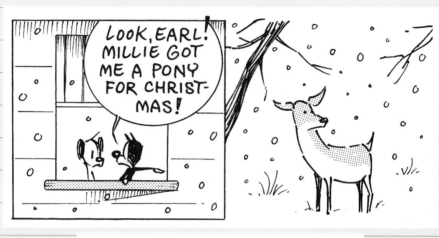

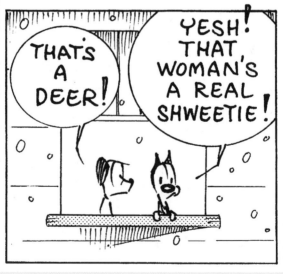

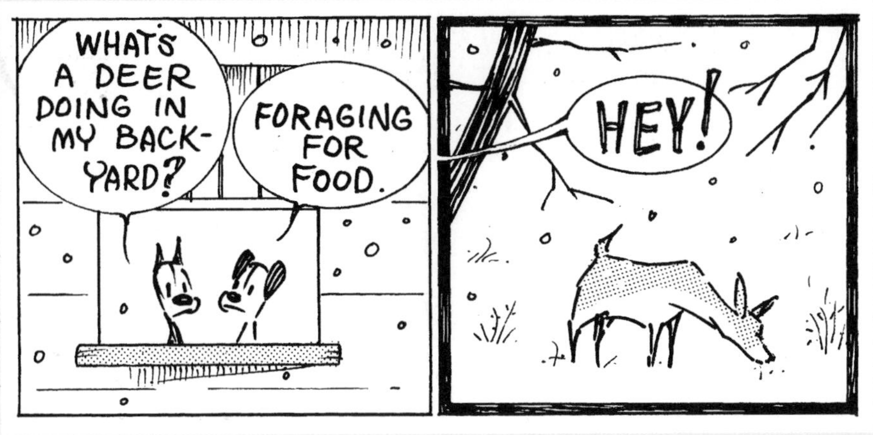
WHAT'S A DEER DOING IN MY BACK-YARD?
FORAGING FOR FOOD.
HEY!

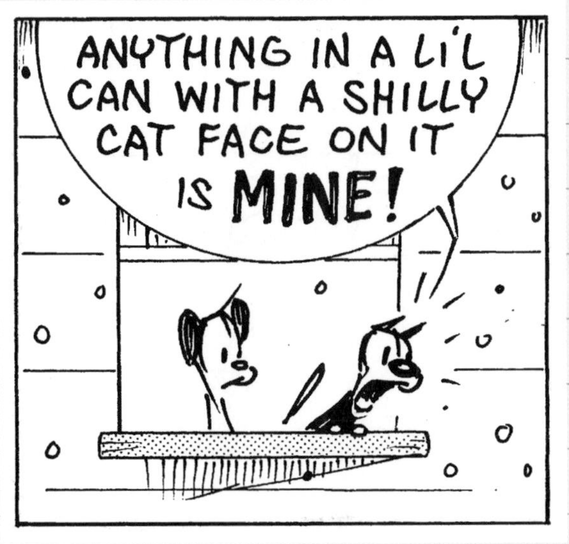
ANYTHING IN A LI'L CAN WITH A SHILLY CAT FACE ON IT IS MINE!

WHAT IS THE DEER 'PROBLEM'?
WHAT ELSE!?! OVER POPULATION. —THERE'S JUST TOO MANY AND NOT ENOUGH SPACE.
YESH...SHOMETIMES THEY CAN BE A NUISANCE.

PEOPLE.

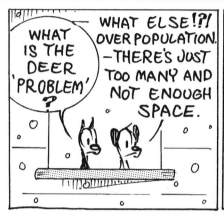

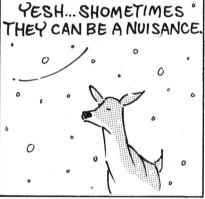

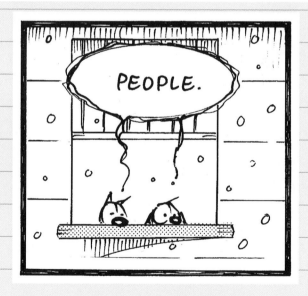

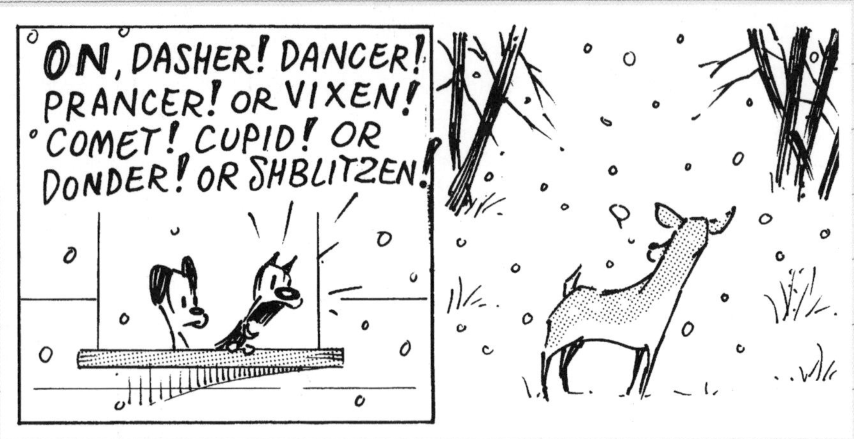
ON, DASHER! DANCER! PRANCER! OR VIXEN! COMET! CUPID! OR DONDER! OR SHBLITZEN!

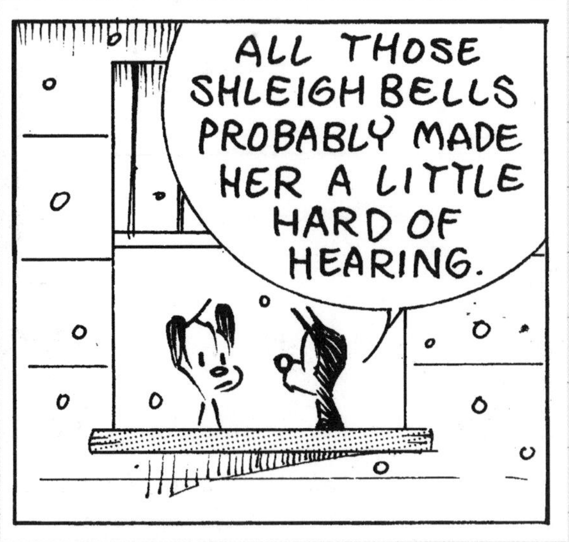
ALL THOSE SHLEIGH BELLS PROBABLY MADE HER A LITTLE HARD OF HEARING.

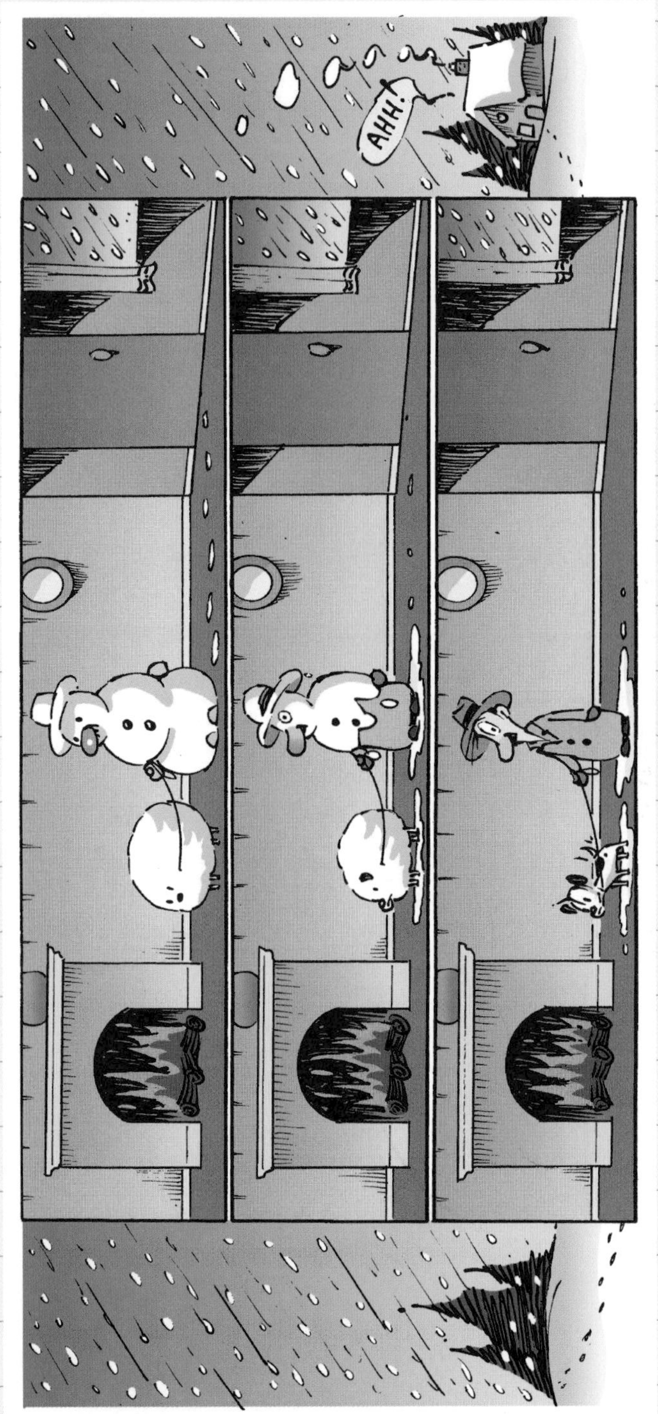
AHH!

SNOW.
YESH.
BONK
BONK

A HEAVY SNOW.
YESH.

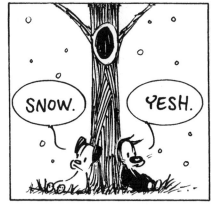

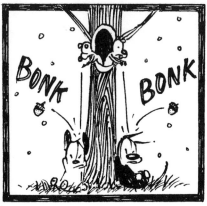

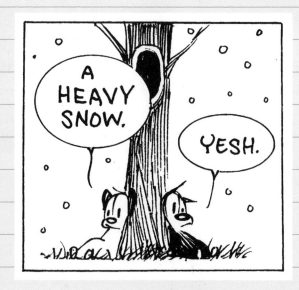

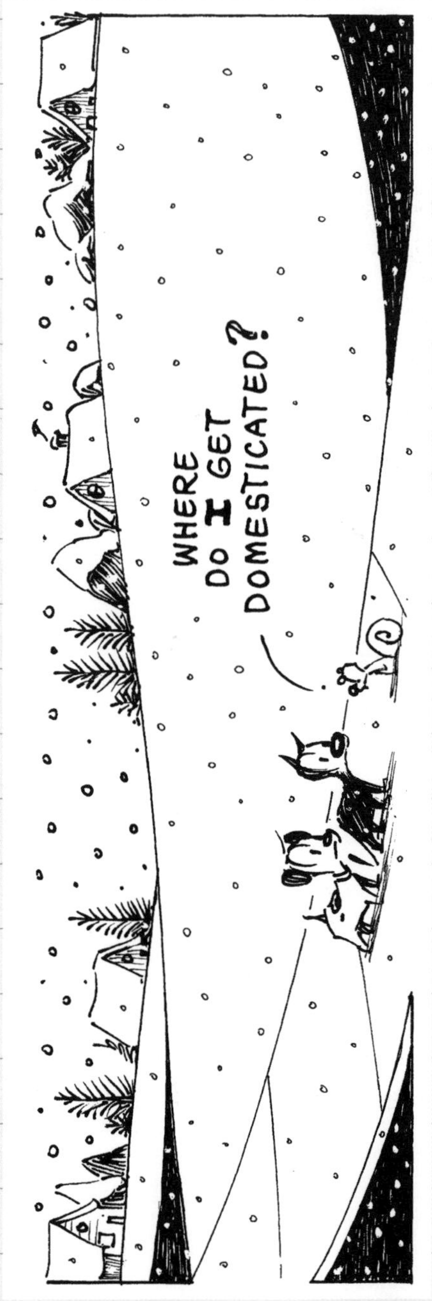
WHERE DO I GET DOMESTICATED?

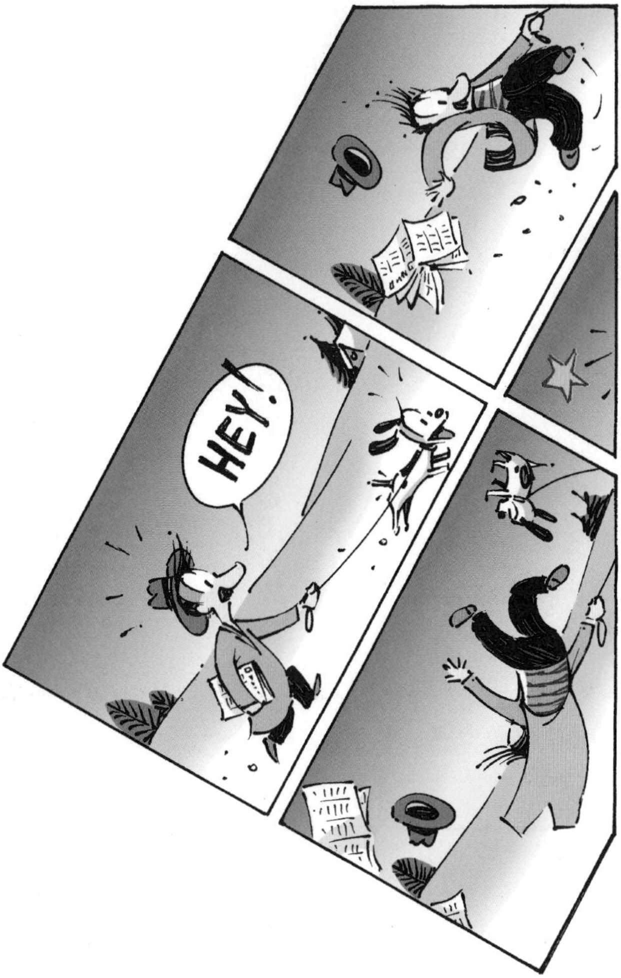
HEY!

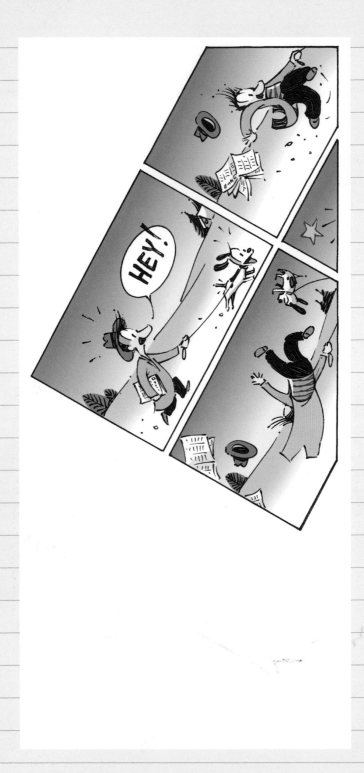

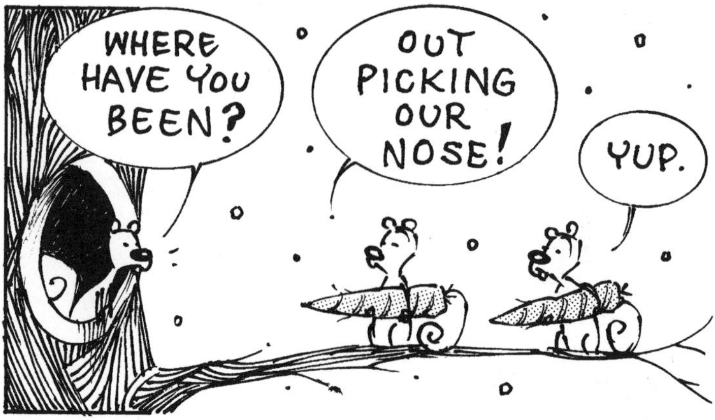
WHERE HAVE YOU BEEN?
OUT PICKING OUR NOSE!
YUP.

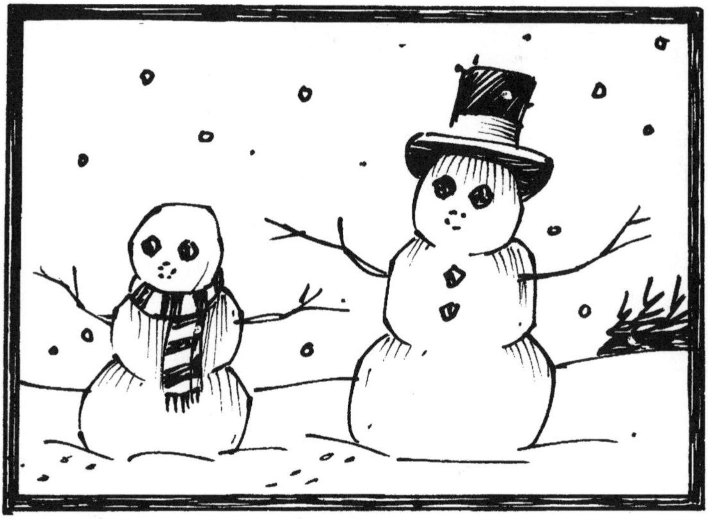

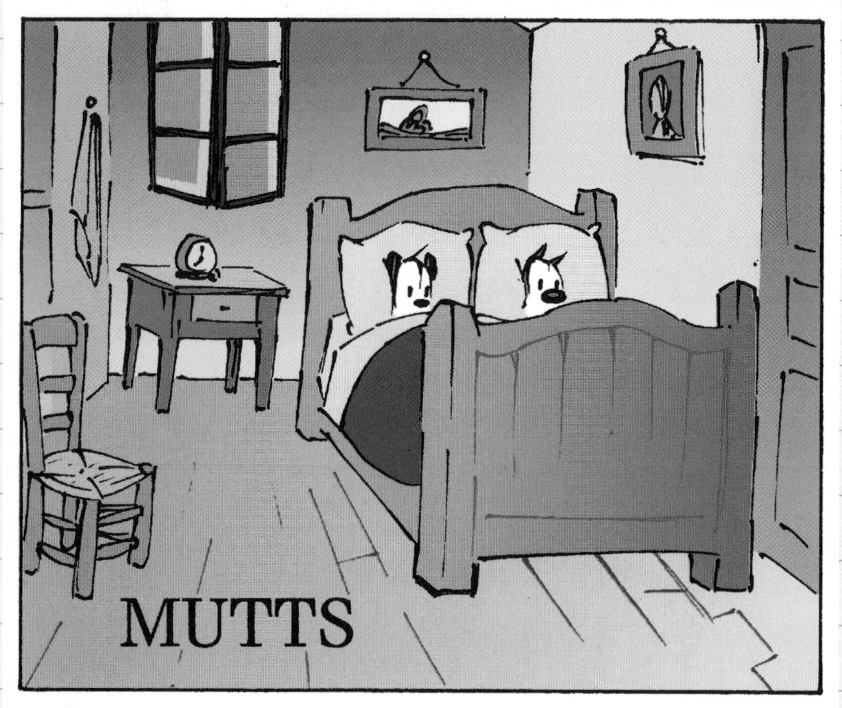
MUTTS

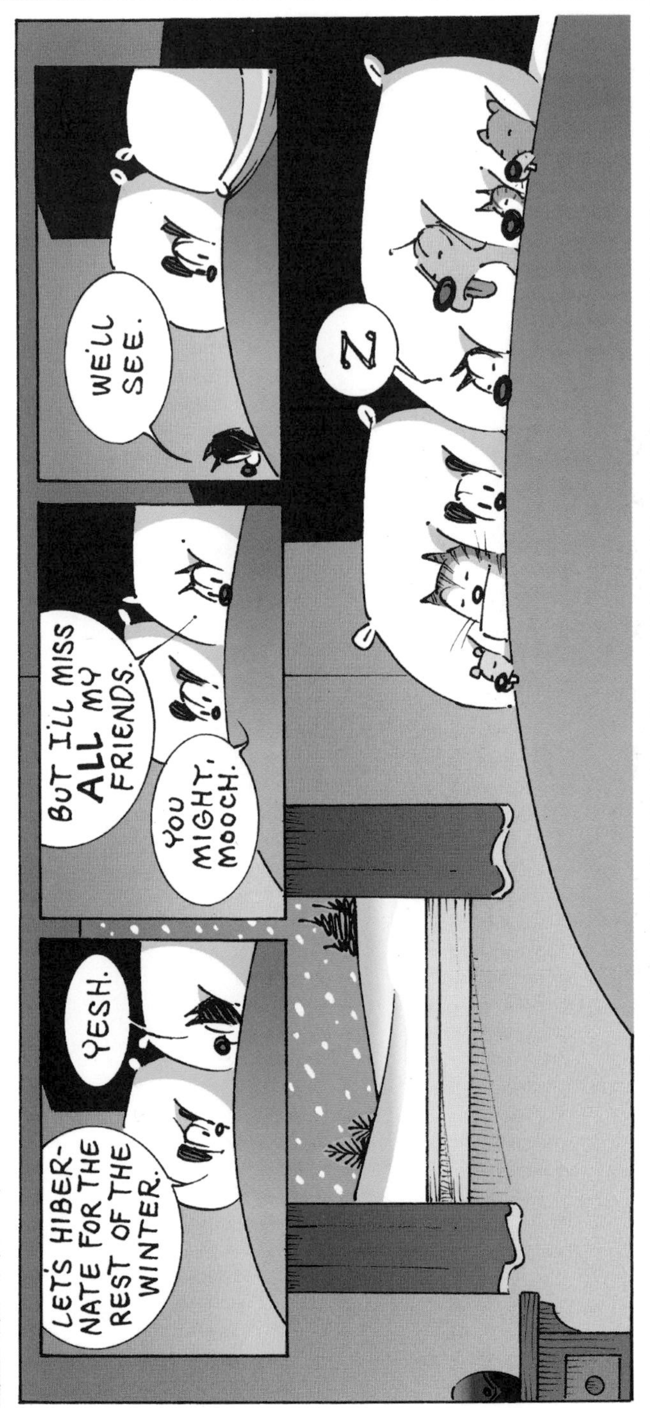
LET'S HIBER-NATE FOR THE REST OF THE WINTER.
YESH.
BUT I'LL MISS ALL MY FRIENDS.
YOU MIGHT, MOOCH.
WE'LL SEE.
Z

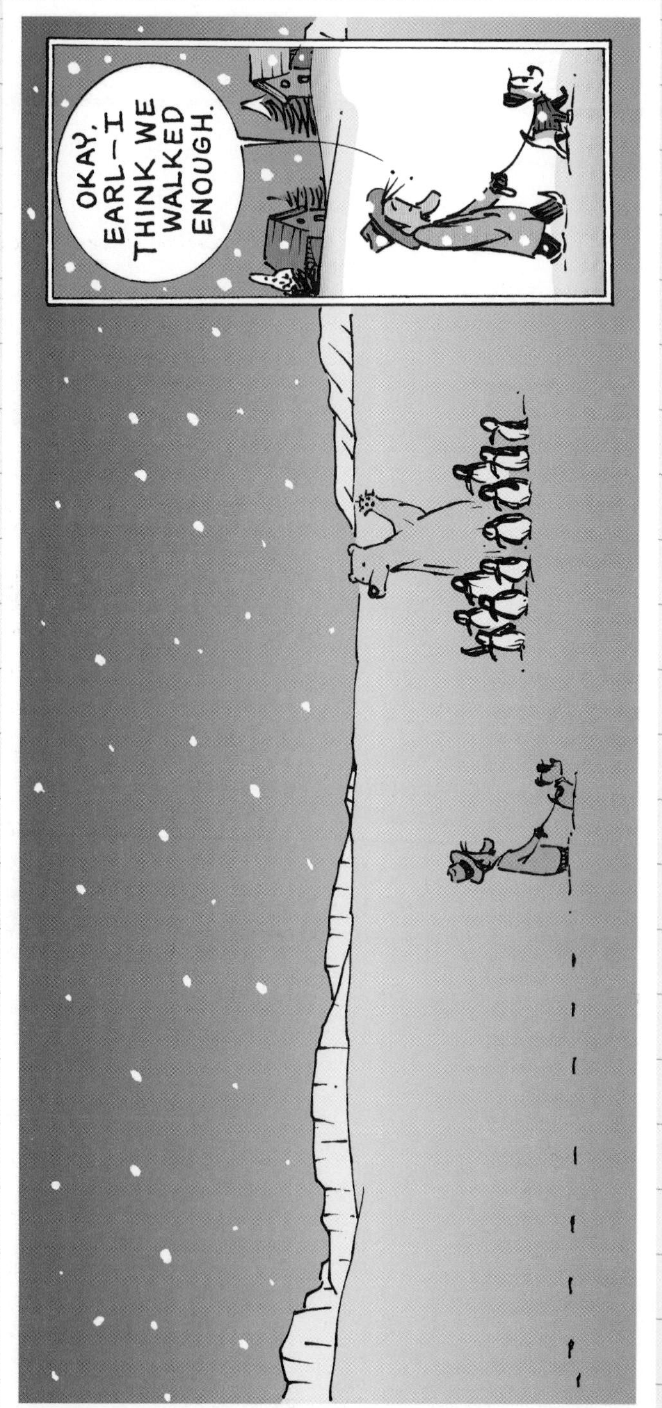
OKAY, EARL—I THINK WE WALKED ENOUGH.

ZIP
BONK
THIS GUY IS
TOO EASY.

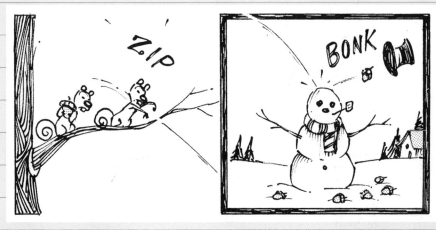

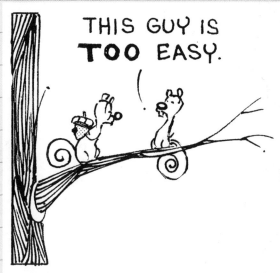

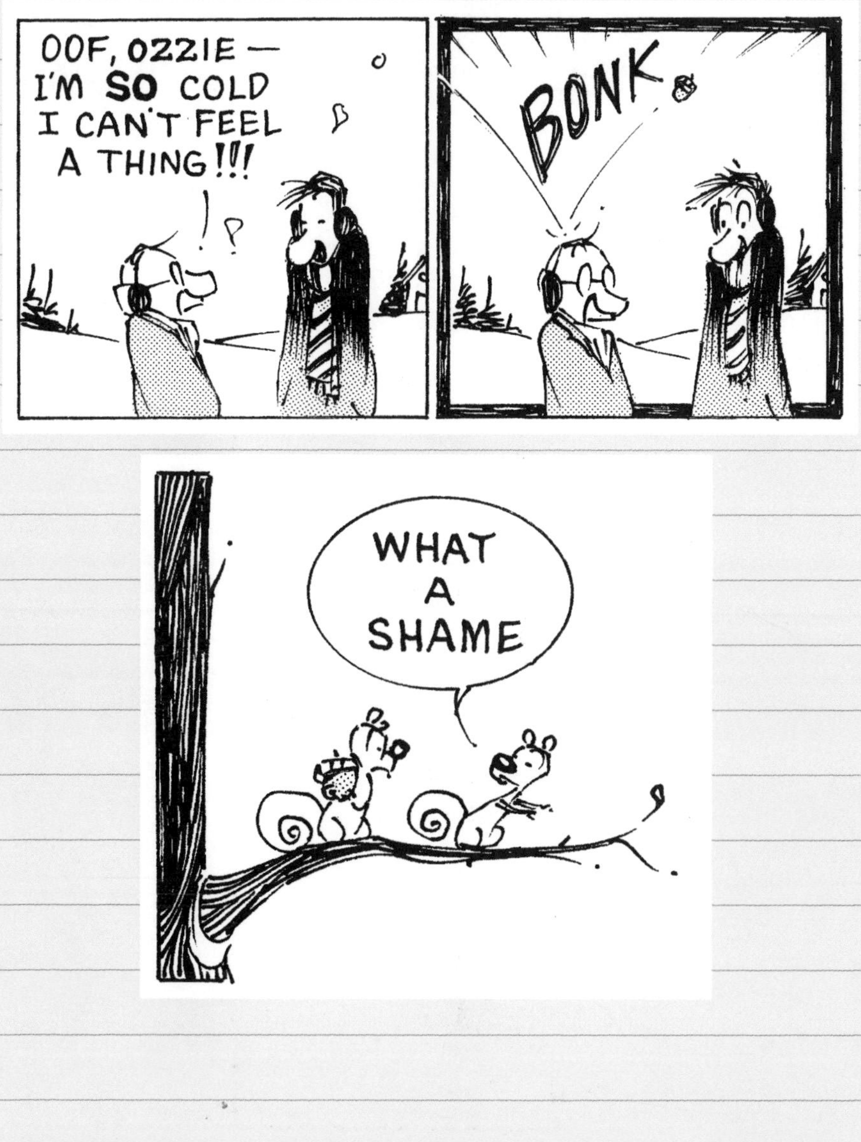
OOF, OZZIE — I'M SO COLD I CAN'T FEEL A THING!!!
!?
BONK
WHAT A SHAME

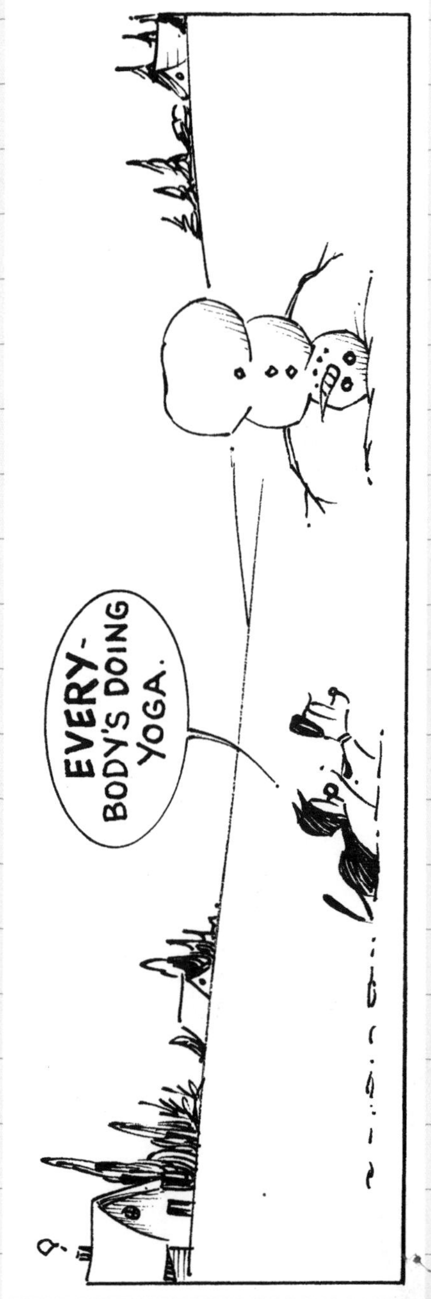
EVERY-BODY'S DOING YOGA.

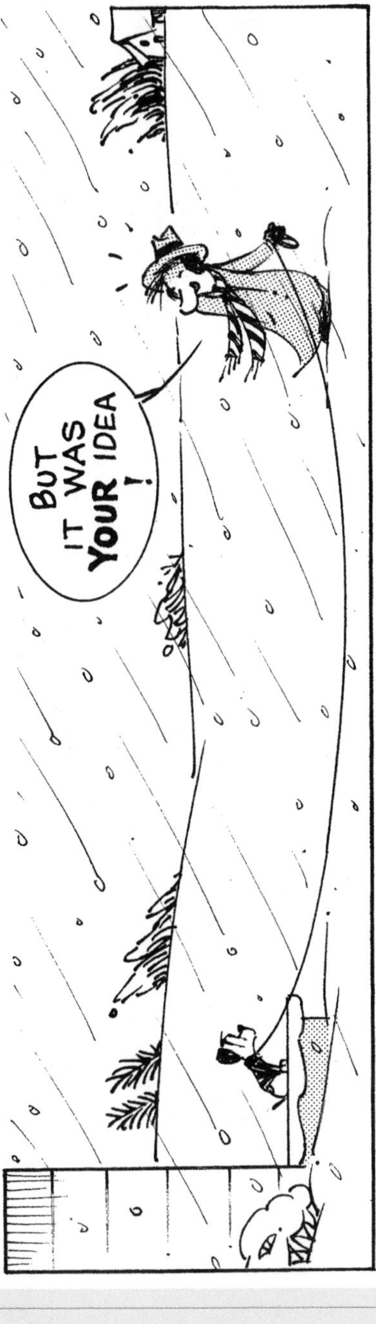
BUT IT WAS **YOUR** IDEA !

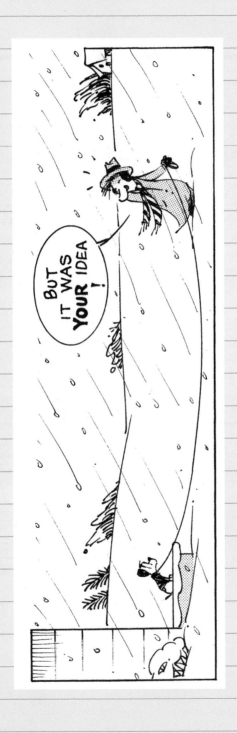

MILLIE— I'M GOING OUT TO SHOVEL A PATH.
HEY!
THE DELI IS THAT WAY!!!

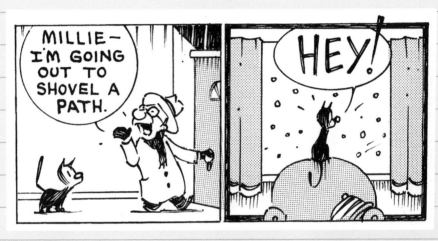

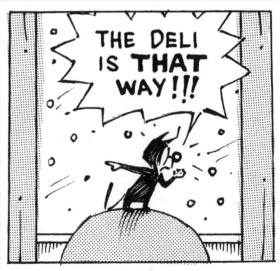

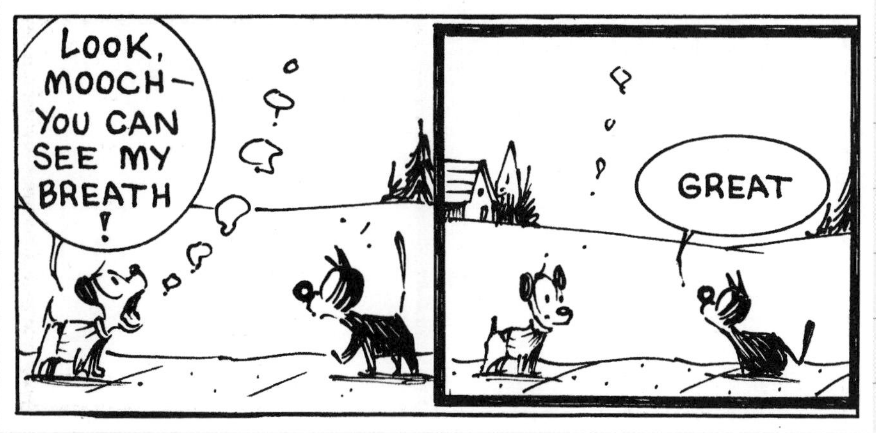
LOOK, MOOCH- YOU CAN SEE MY BREATH!
GREAT

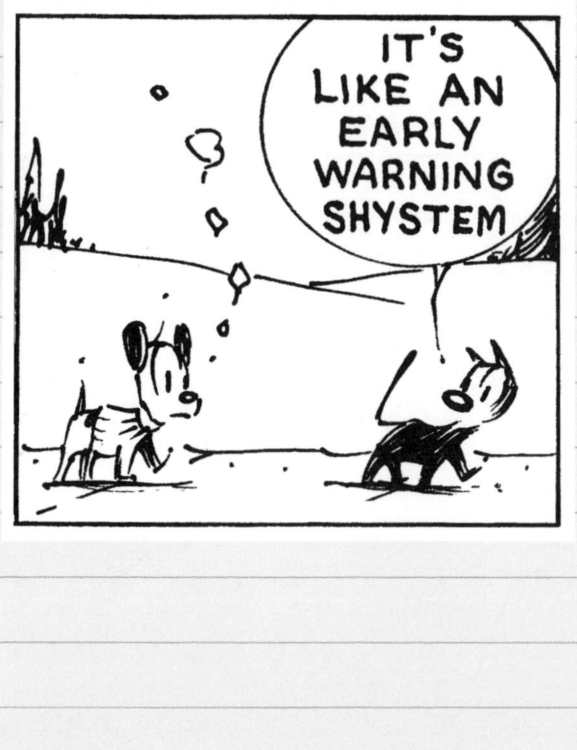
IT'S LIKE AN EARLY WARNING SHYSTEM

I DON'T MIND A FEW FLAKES BUT THEN THEY HAVE To SHTOP!
NOBODY LISTENS.

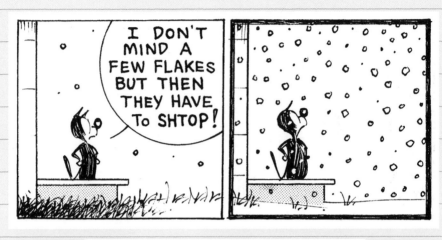

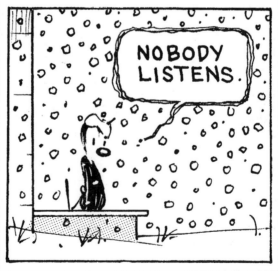

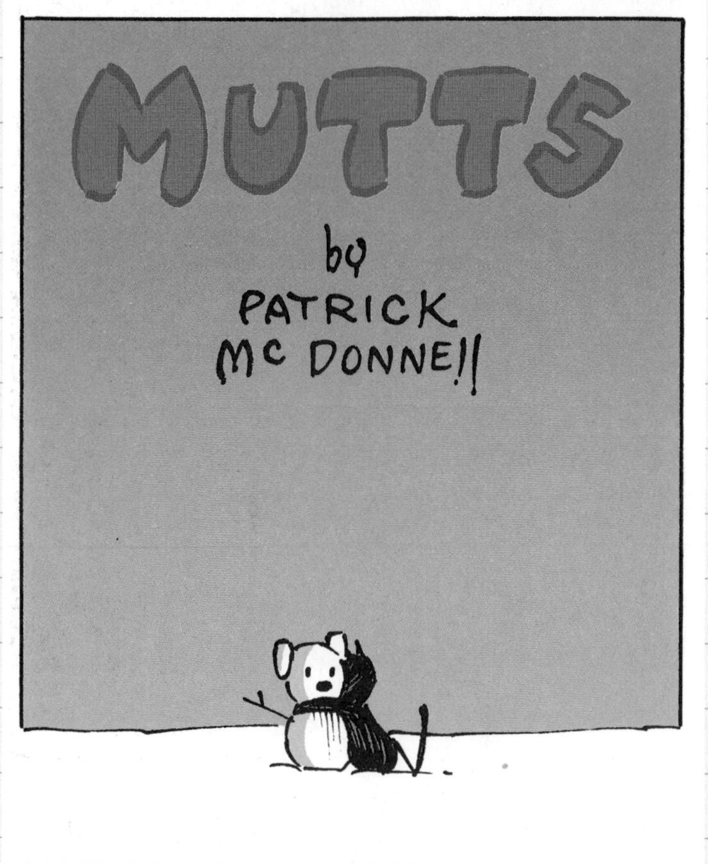
MUTTS
by
PATRICK
MC DONNELL

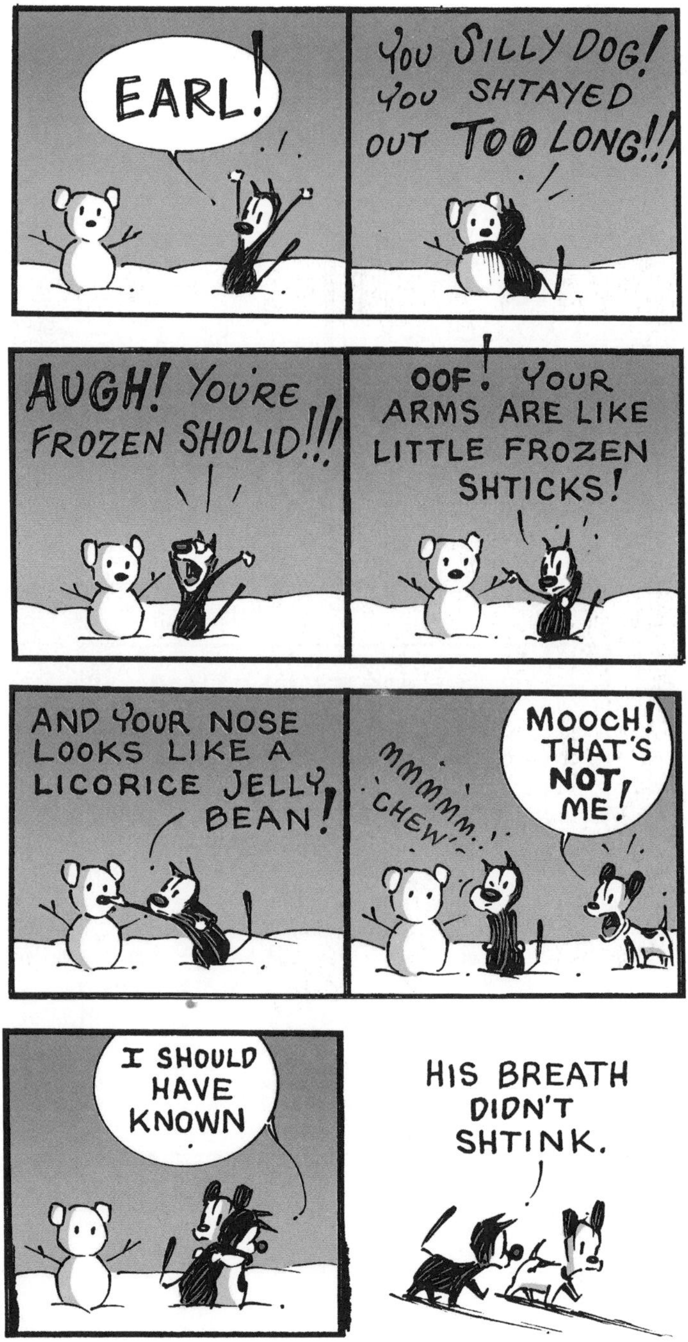
EARL!
YOU SILLY DOG! YOU SHTAYED OUT TOO LONG!!!
AUGH! YOU'RE FROZEN SHOLID!!!
OOF! YOUR ARMS ARE LIKE LITTLE FROZEN SHTICKS!
AND YOUR NOSE LOOKS LIKE A LICORICE JELLY BEAN!
MMMMM...
CHEW
MOOCH! THAT'S NOT ME!
I SHOULD HAVE KNOWN.
HIS BREATH DIDN'T SHTINK.

THE WEATHERMAN SAYS THE SNOW WILL STOP AT TWO O'CLOCK
THE NERVE
TELL HIM TO SHMAKE IT TEN-THIRTY!

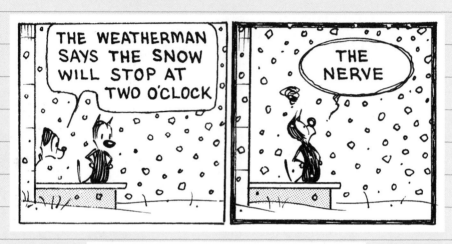

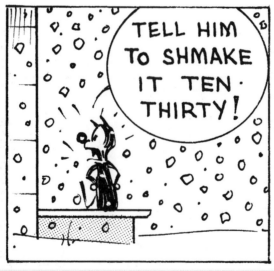

WHAT DOES THAT DOPEY WEATHERMAN SAY NOW !?!
HE SAYS IT COULD GET "NASTY."
WHA...!?!
HE SHTARTED IT!

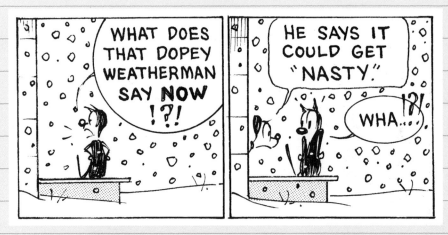

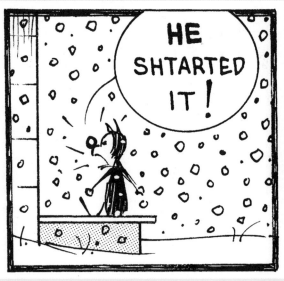

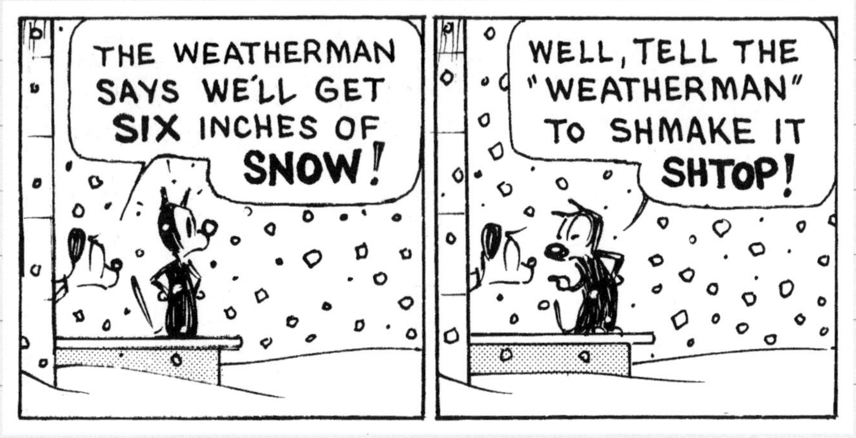
THE WEATHERMAN SAYS WE'LL GET SIX INCHES OF SNOW!
WELL, TELL THE "WEATHERMAN" TO SHMAKE IT SHTOP!

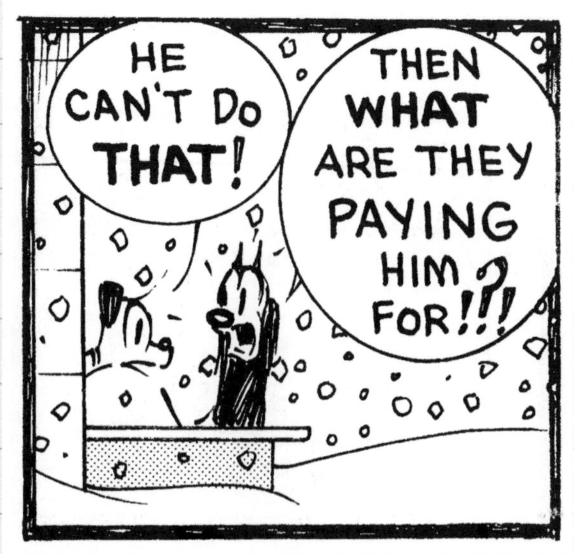
HE CAN'T DO THAT!
THEN WHAT ARE THEY PAYING HIM FOR?!?!

MOOCH! THERE'S THE WEATHERMAN DOING A LIVE REMOTE.
HA! JUST LIKE I SAID IT WOULD— SIX INCHES OF SNOW!
HA! HA!

SHPLAT

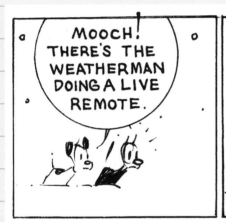

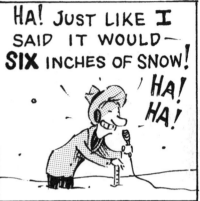

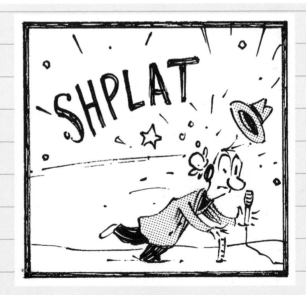

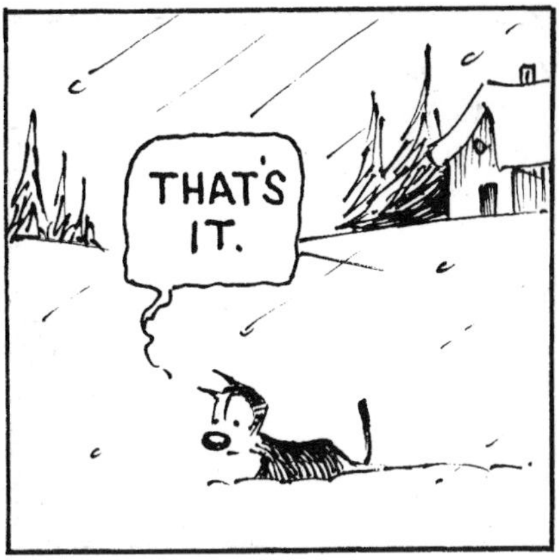
THAT'S IT.

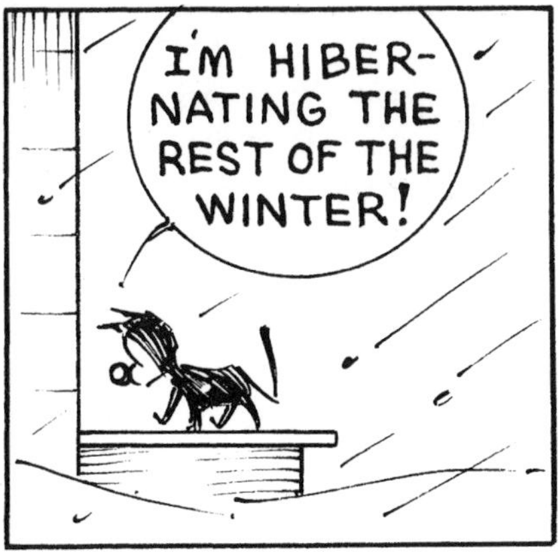
I'M HIBERNATING THE REST OF THE WINTER!

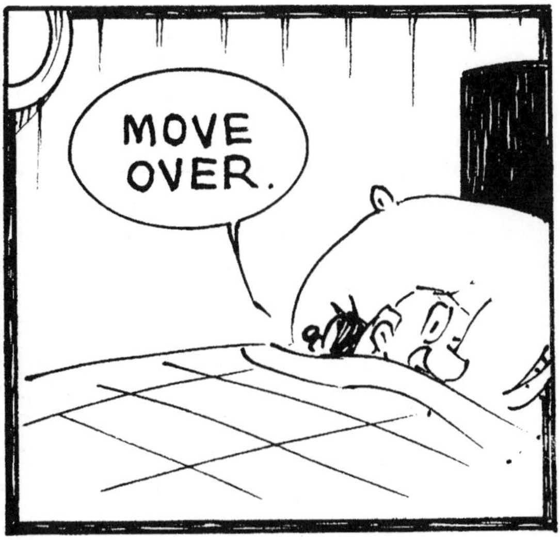
MOVE OVER.

YUM!
HOW WAS DOOZY'S SNOW-MAN?
HIS NOSE WAS RUNNING.

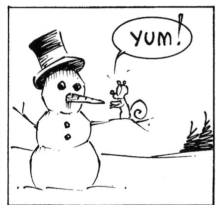

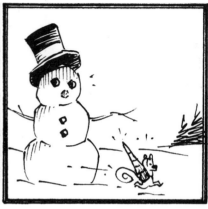

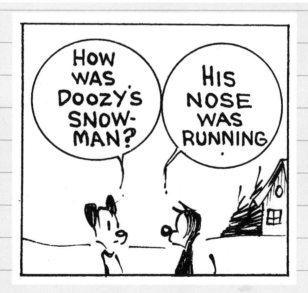

LOOK MOOCH, DOOZY BUILT AN IGLOO.
WHAT'S AN IGLOO?
A HOUSE MADE OF SNOW!
TURN UP THE THERMOSTAT.

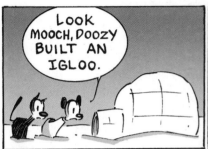

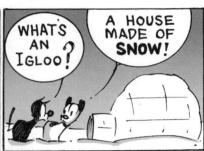

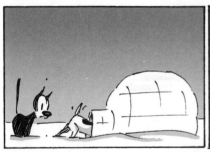

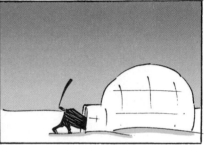

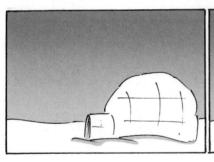

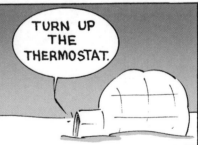

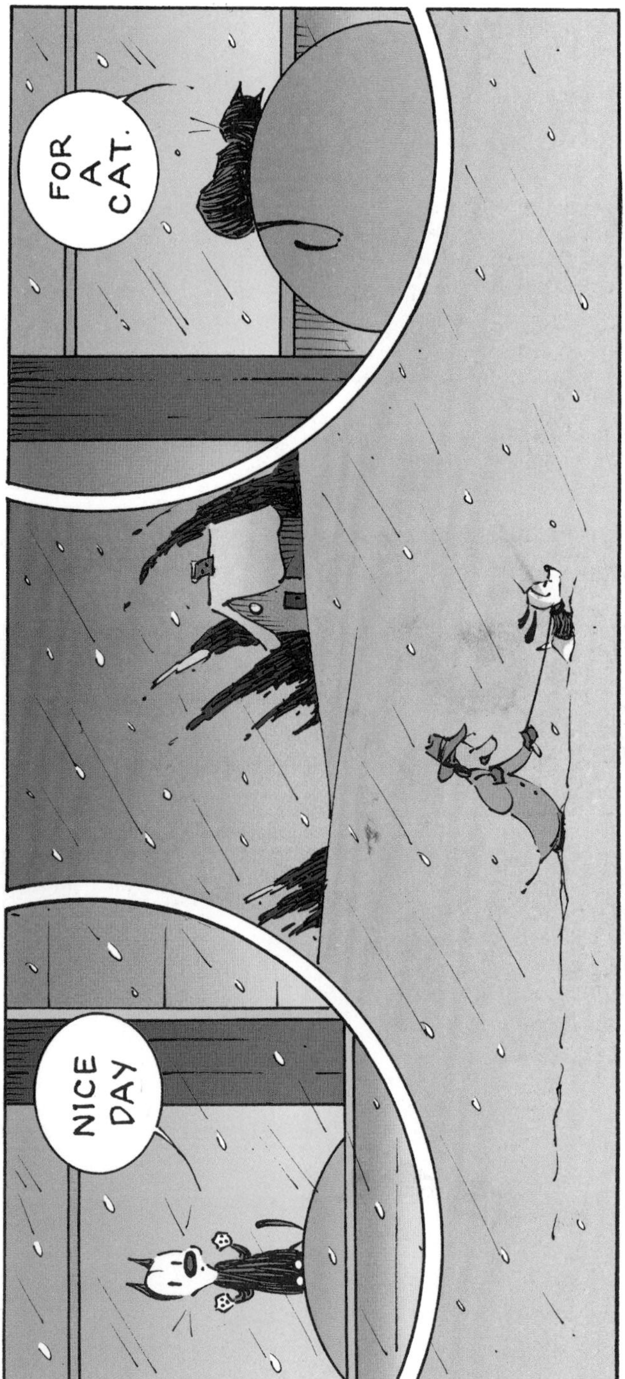
NICE DAY
FOR A CAT.

SO, WUZZY, TRYING TO DO SOME HEAVY-DUTY SHLEEPING - ARE WE?
HERE - WATCH A PRO.
Z
zZZZ
AHH- RISE AND SHINE! I'M GOOD TO GO!! EVERYBODY UP!!!
I "POWER" HIBERNATE

THAT WAS SOME SNOW LAST NIGHT. DO WE HAVE ENOUGH TO GET BY?
YES... BUT WE'RE A LITTLE LOW ON CAT FOOD.

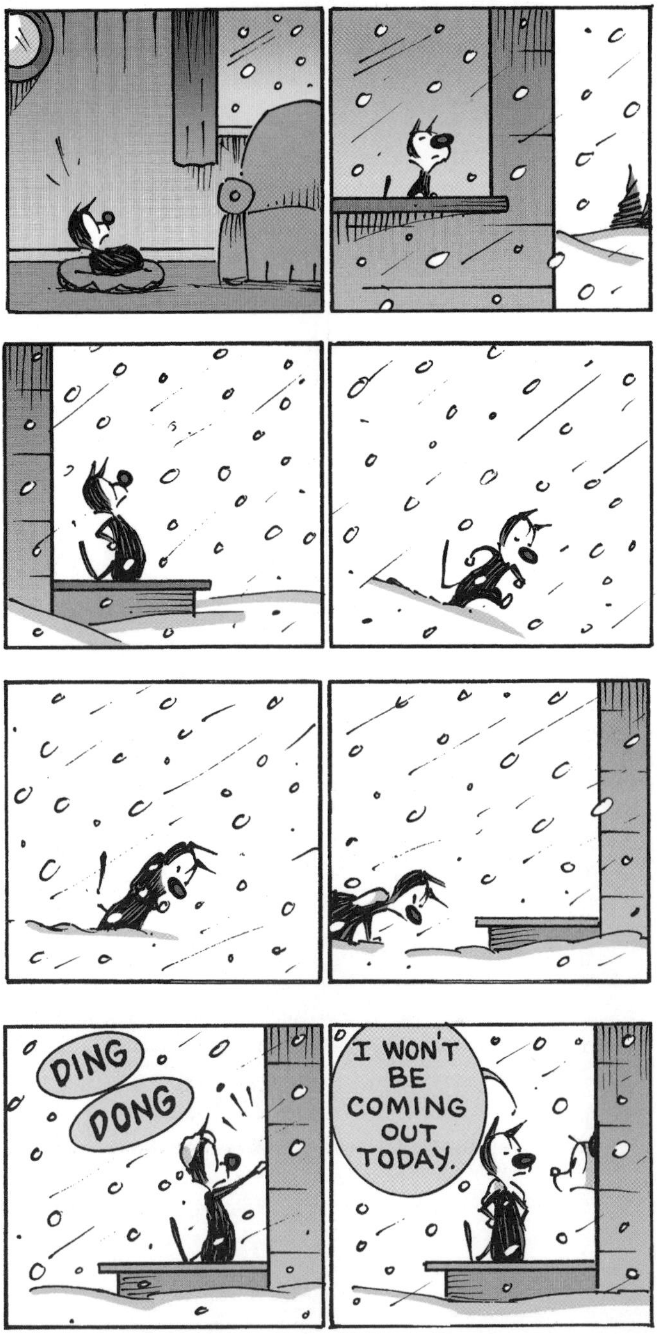
DING
DONG
I WON'T BE COMING OUT TODAY.

THIS IS MY "IT'S TOO COLD TO GO OUTSIDE" FACE
...AND THIS IS MY "IT'S TOO COLD TO GO OUTSIDE" FACE ...OUTSIDE!!!

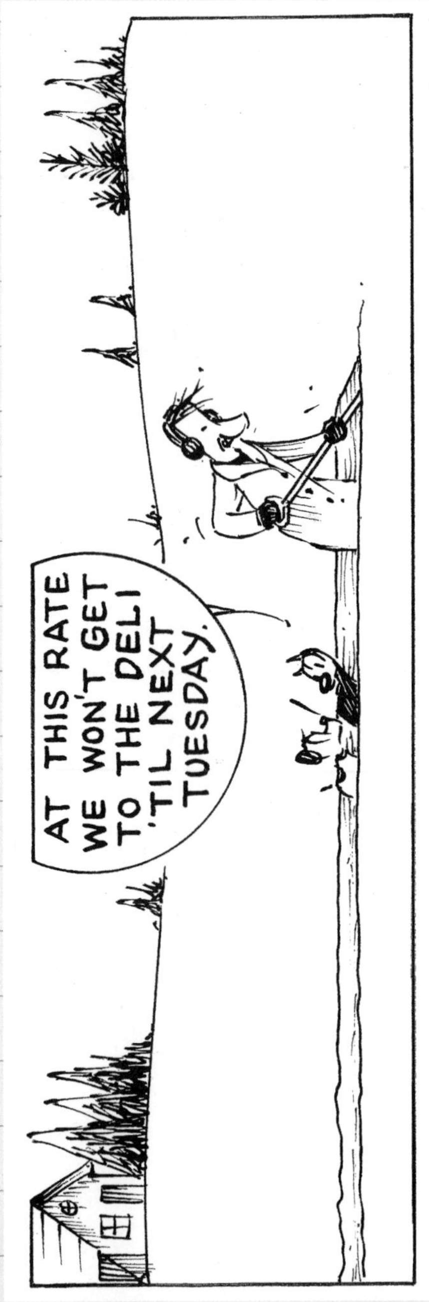
AT THIS RATE WE WON'T GET TO THE DELI 'TIL NEXT TUESDAY.

HEY, EARL, LET'S GO FOR A BOING!

BOING
BOING
BOING

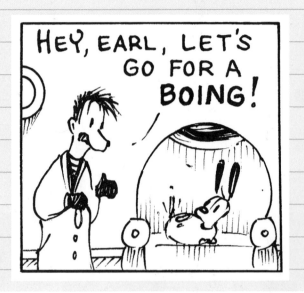

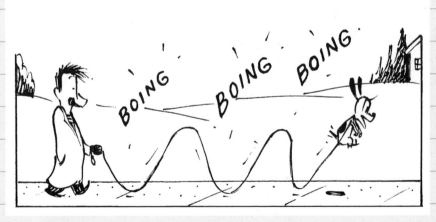

I CAN'T WAIT TO SHOW EARL!
I HAVE SHCIENTIFIC HISTORY RIGHT HERE IN MY HANDS!!!
TWO IDENTICAL SHNOW-FLAKES!!!
VOILÀ!
LOOKS LIKE TWO TINY PUDDLES.
YESH
BUT SHTILL UNCANNILY SIMILAR.

IT'S TIME TO SHTART THIS DAY!
ZZZZ...

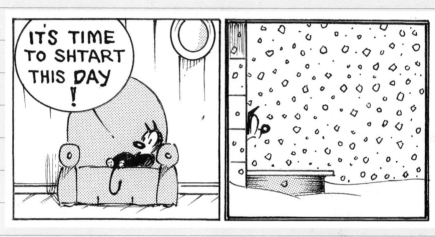

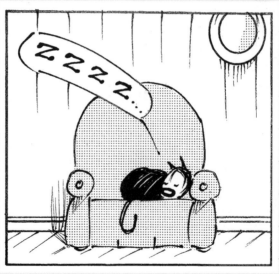

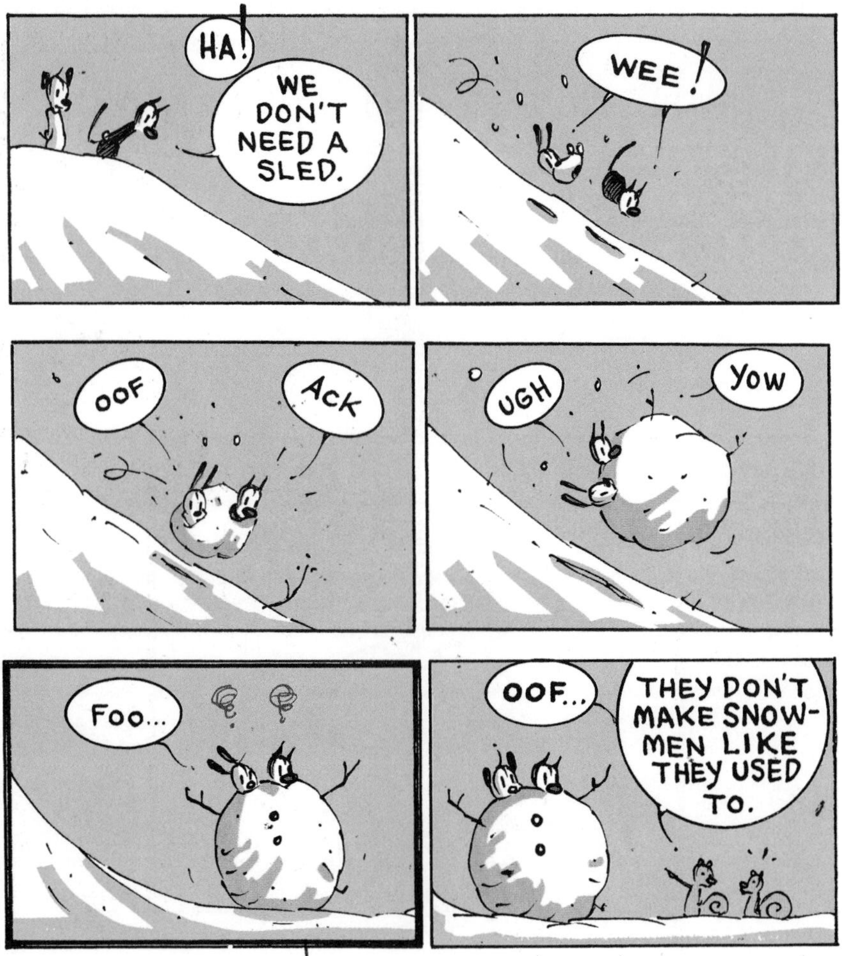
HA!
WE DON'T NEED A SLED.
WEE!
OOF
ACK
UGH
YOW
FOO...
OOF...
THEY DON'T MAKE SNOW-MEN LIKE THEY USED TO.

WOOFIE WUVS SNOW
PLOOPF
...AND SNOW WUVS WOOFIE!

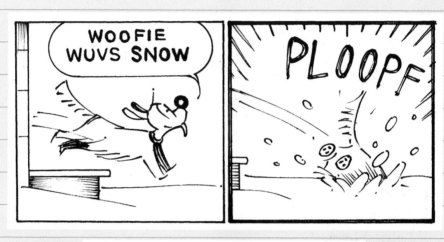

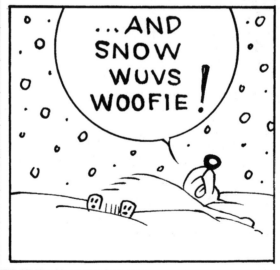

MORE SHNOW!?!
YEESH.
I THOUGHT THEY'D RUN OUT OF FLAKES BY NOW.

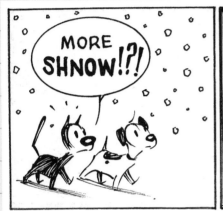

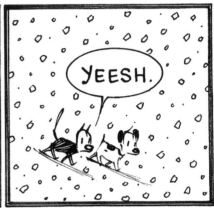

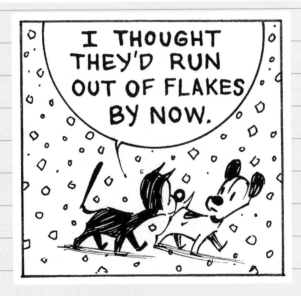

I LOVE MY TEDDY.

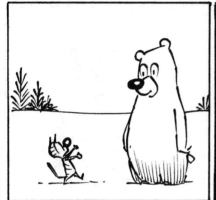

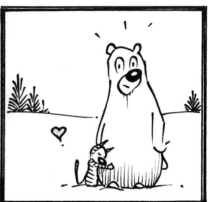

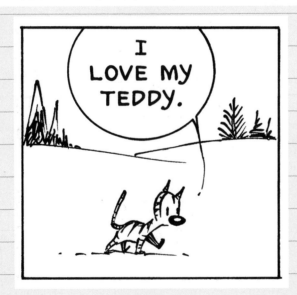

WHOA.
THAT'S ONE STUFFED BEAR!

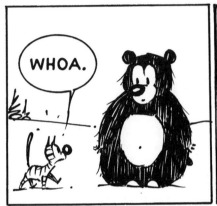

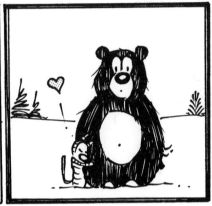

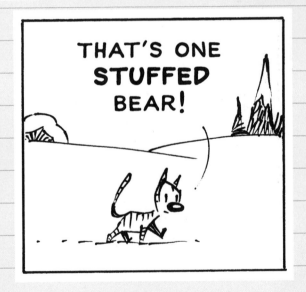

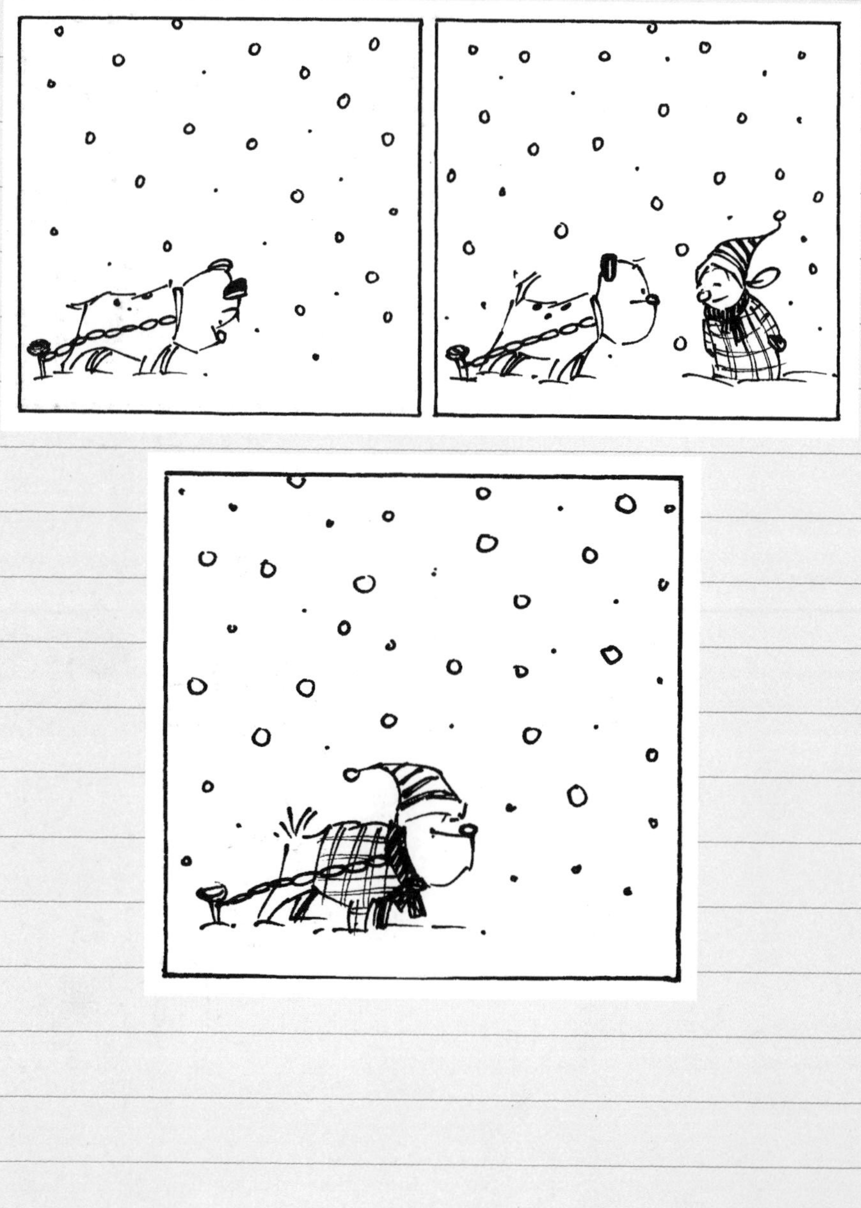

I'M BORED.
WELL, WHY DON'T YOU JUST FLY AWAY?
DUH.
HA
HA
HA
WHY DIDN'T I THINK OF THAT!
!
!
!

A PENGUIN!?!
HOW DID YOU GET HERE!?!
I FLEW.
PENGUINS DON'T FLY!!!
I DIDN'T SAY IT WAS EASY!

YOU SAID YOU FLEW HERE!?!
YES.
BUT I DON'T BELIEVE PENGUINS CAN FLY!
I KNOW.
BUT I DO.

SURE, I CAN FLY — I JUST FLAP MY WINGS REAL HARD!
FWIP
FWIP
FWAP
AND... VOILÀ — I'M FLYING!!!
TWO INCHES OFF THE GROUND!?!
WHAT KIND OF FLYING IS THAT!?!
BREATH-TAKING!

WHO SAYS PENGUINS CAN'T FLY—LOOK AT ME GO!–BACK TO THE POLE! S'LONG, FELLOWS!
WOW!
LOOK AT THAT VIEW!!!

"BIRD'S EYE"

PHEW
I'M BACK!
FOO...
WATTATRIP!
BUT PENGUINS DON'T FLY!!!
YES
AND NOW I KNOW WHY.

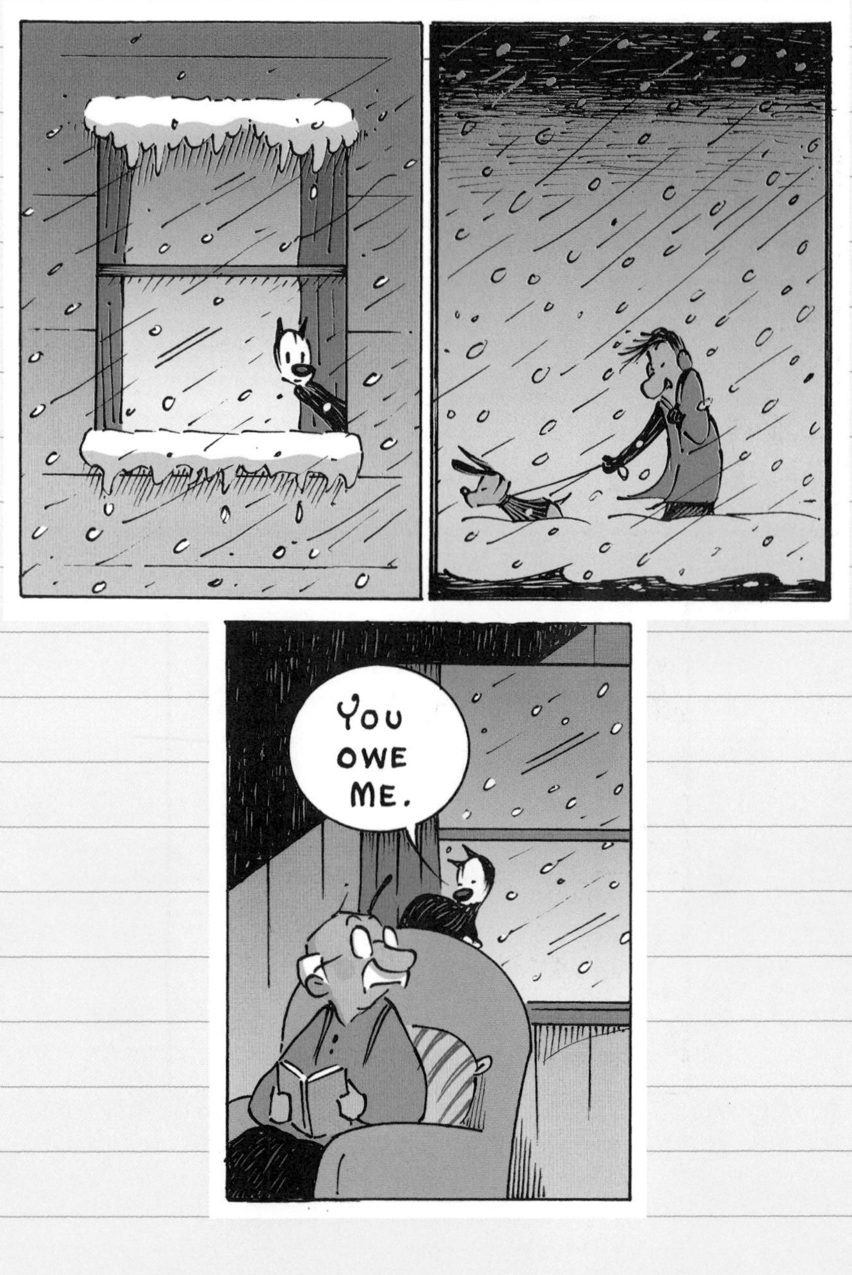
YOU OWE ME.

WHAT'S ON MY HOLIDAY LIST THIS YEAR?
1. LOVE EVERYONE
OOOH...
THAT'S A BIG LIST.

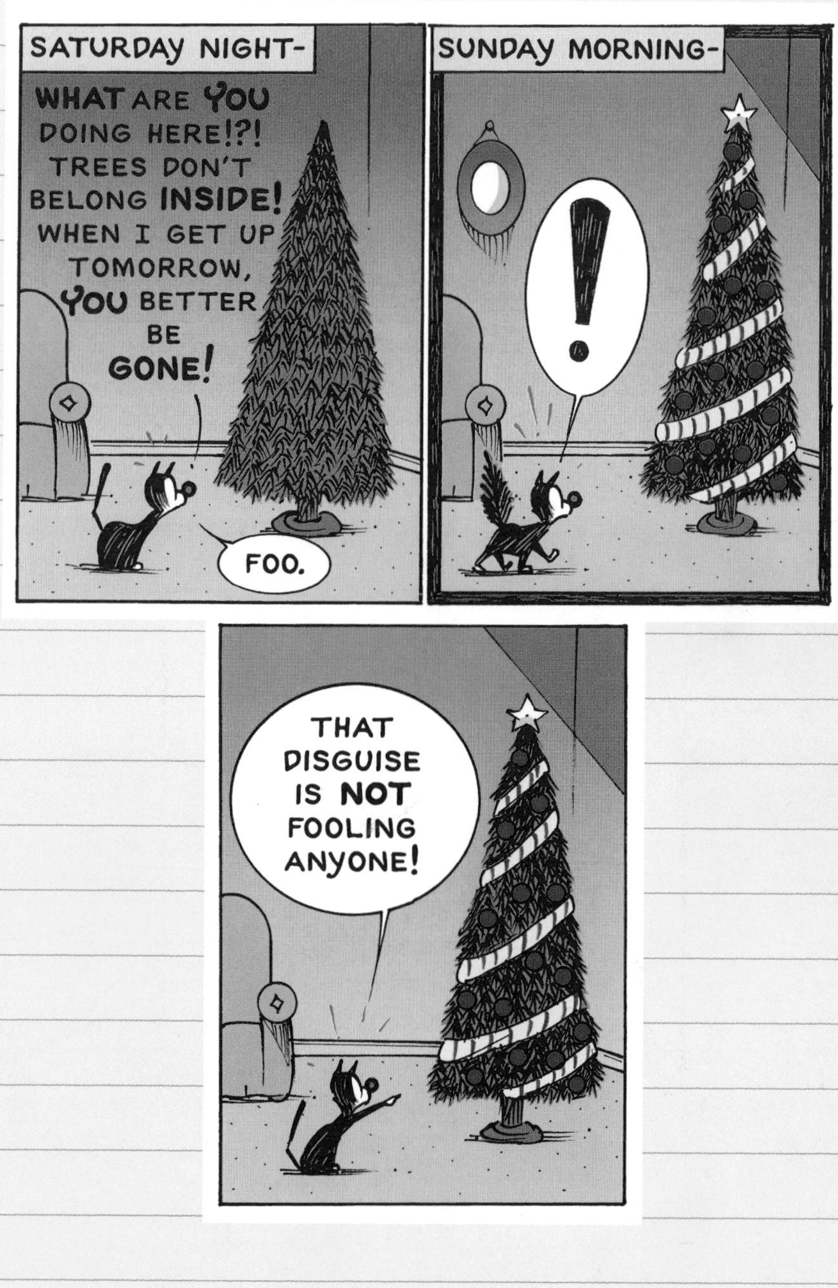
SATURDAY NIGHT-
WHAT ARE YOU DOING HERE!?! TREES DON'T BELONG INSIDE! WHEN I GET UP TOMORROW, YOU BETTER BE GONE!
FOO.
SUNDAY MORNING-
!
THAT DISGUISE IS NOT FOOLING ANYONE!

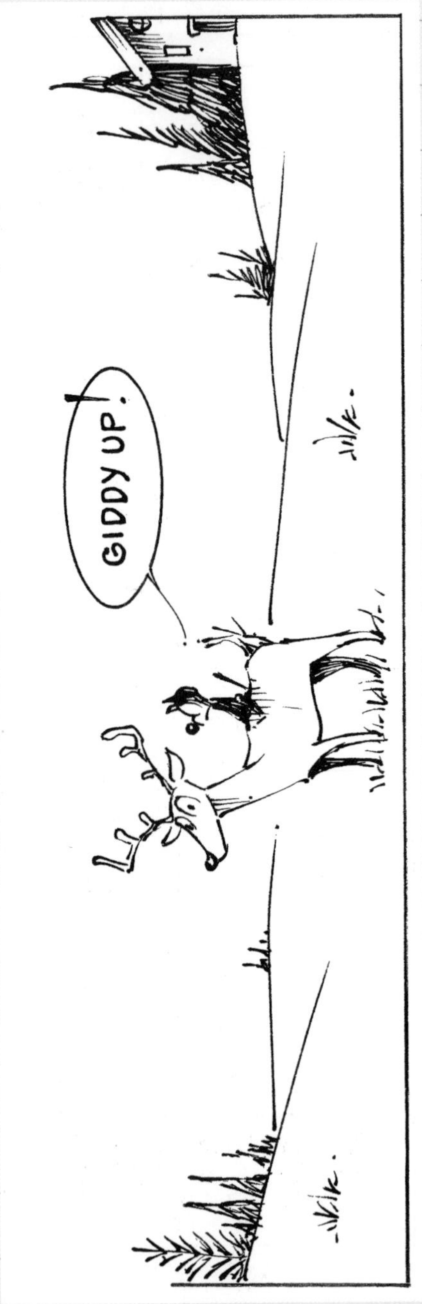
GIDDY UP!

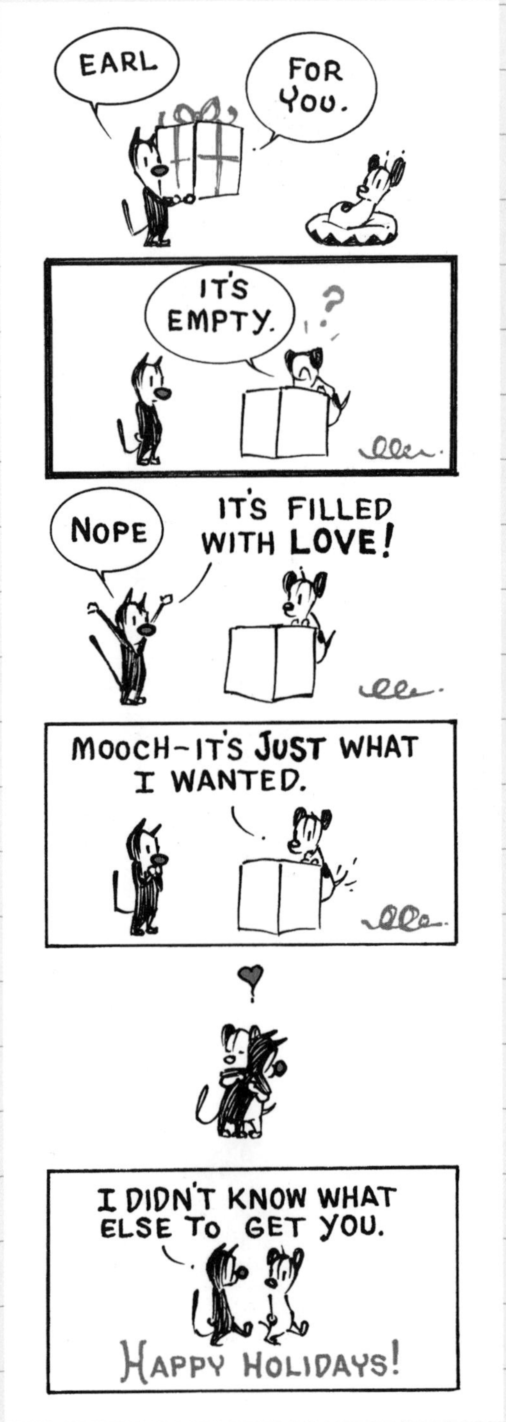
EARL
FOR YOU.
IT'S EMPTY.
?
NOPE
IT'S FILLED WITH LOVE!
MOOCH-IT'S JUST WHAT I WANTED.
I DIDN'T KNOW WHAT ELSE TO GET YOU.
HAPPY HOLIDAYS!

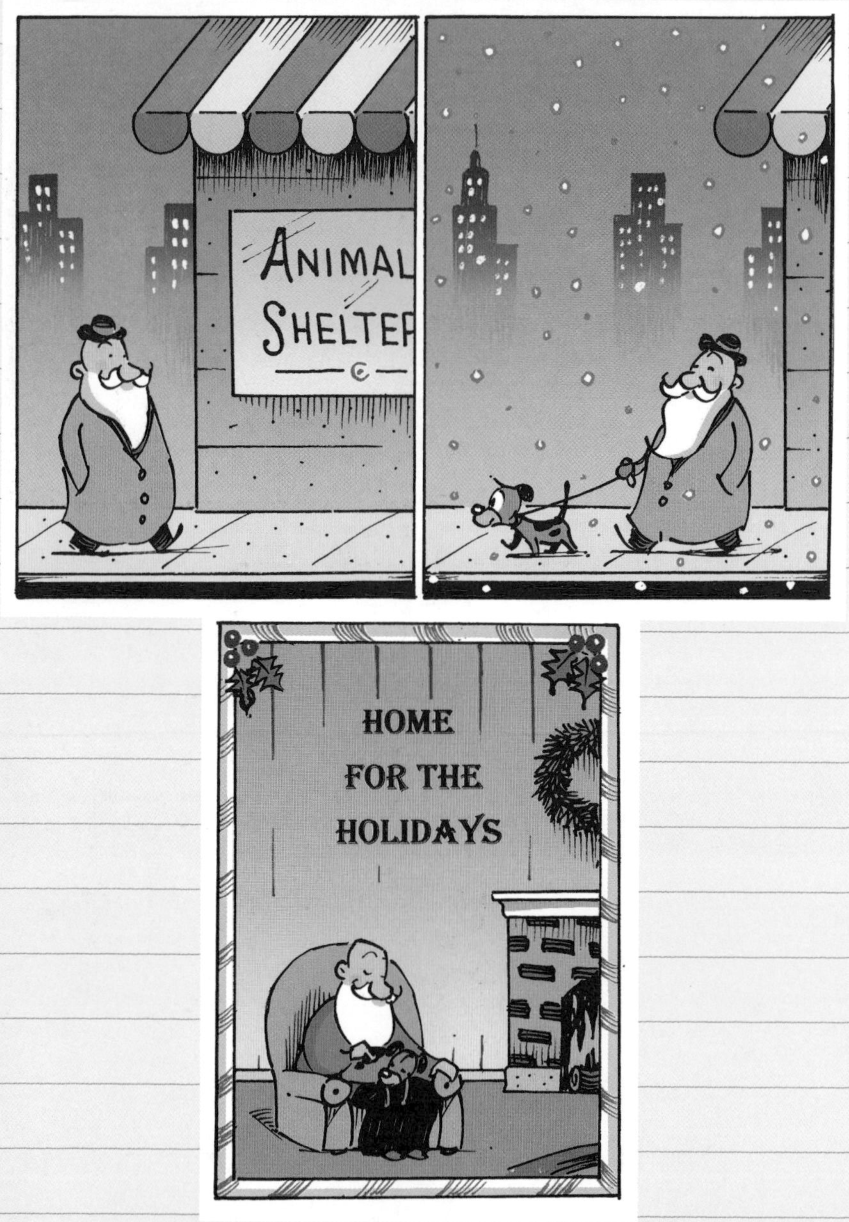
ANIMAL
SHELTE
HOME
FOR THE
HOLIDAYS

PURRK!
JOY TO THE WORLD

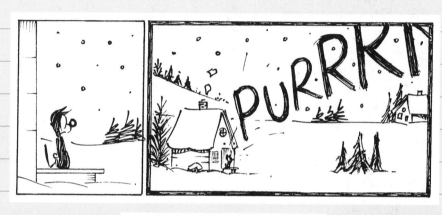

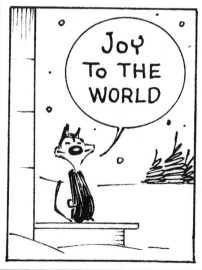

WHEN'S SHUMMER VACATION?

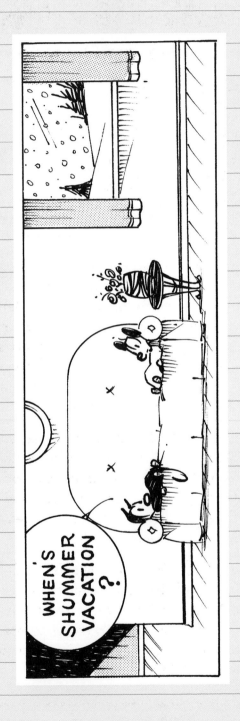

MORE TO EXPLORE! Learn how you can help your animal friends!

The Winter Outside

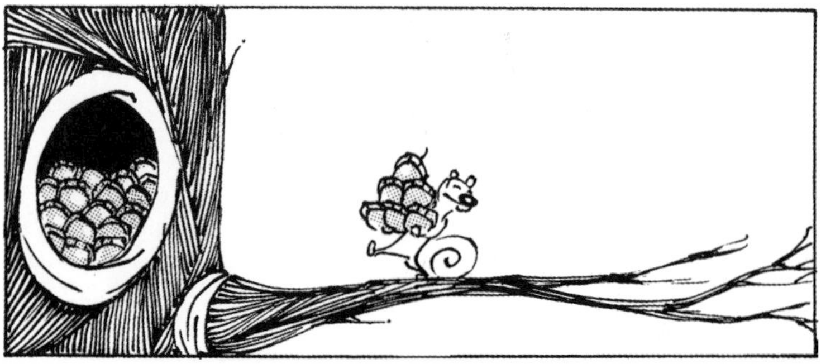

It is a beautiful and magical time when winter rolls around. As the world outside grows hush under the sleepy blanket of the season, why not consider how some animals are getting along keeping warm and fed? Here are some facts from our good friends at The Humane Society of the United States about some critters that may be in your local area, and how you can help animals in the winter months:

- **Gray squirrels** build watertight winter nests using up to 26 layers of flattened, dried leaves, lining the inside with shredded inner bark from dead trees. In winter, they gather the acorns, nuts, and maple seeds that they buried in the fall, and feed on tree buds and bark as backup foods.

- **Downy woodpeckers** frequently like to flock with other species of birds, increasing both their safety from predators, and their chances of finding food. For shelter, downy woodpeckers dig roosts in tree cavities, using wood strips from from the inside of the tree as bedding.

- In preparation for the months ahead, **raccoons** spend the summer and autumn eating to build up fat stores for insulation against the cold. Through the course of the winter, it is common for raccoons to burn off between 14 and 50 percent of their body weight! They also adapt to lower temperatures by growing thicker fur coats. But even so, raccoons tend to spend most of the winter snuggled up with their tails in their dens.

- **Chipmunks** hibernate for the winter, but unlike raccoons and squirrels, they do not store fat. They instead spend the fall months gathering a supply of seeds, nuts, grains, and fruit to munch on whenever they get hungry. Did you know that baby squirrels spend only two months feeding from what their parents gather before they begin to collect their own food for winter?

The winter can be a rough time for those without the luxury of comfy sweaters or a warm home with regular din-din. Here are some ways you can lend a hand in your own backyard:

- A good start would be to consider going green for the holidays by planting seeds in your yard! Winter is the perfect time to start seedlings of native plants, bushes, and trees in preparation for the spring. Check online or at a local garden center to find native plants for your region and ask a parent or guardian to help you find the best seeds for your home!

- 🐾 It is helpful to leave dead flowers and plants in the garden beds or in pots until springtime. Just because a flower has lost its beauty, doesn't mean it has outlived its usefulness. The stalks, leaves, and seed heads provide food and protection to all sorts of wildlife. Critters will go especially wild for large flowers like black-eyed Susans, purple coneflowers, and sunflowers, as well as zinnias, marigolds, and cosmos.

- 🐾 **Bats** help the environment as pollinators and seed dispersers. They also help keep the bugs out of your face! Bats are fascinating animals to observe. Look in the evenings to see them swooping though the air to catch mosquitoes! Sadly, bats have recently been having a hard time finding natural homes in the wild. A bat house can really help these cuties out.

- 🐾 Build a winter bird restaurant, and stock it with seeds of your choosing. Bird feeders let you watch birds in your own yard and give the birds food to munch on throughout the winter. Birds appreciate a variety of feeders and the most important thing to do is to keep them full. If you leave home for vacation, ask a friend or neighbor to fill your feeders, especially when cold temperatures and snow is expected. Remember to place your bird restaurant a bit away from your home so the birds will have room to fly about.

Did you know that cats are America's most popular pets? Although Mooch likes to explore the outdoors with his pals, it is really best for your cat to stay indoors where it is safe from the hazards and harms of the bustling outside world. Not every cat has an Earl to keep them out of trouble.

If you'd like to learn more about animals and how you can help them, you can read The Humane Society's Kind News online. Go to humanesociety.org/kindnews and see the most recent stories.

Stay Warm!

Mutts is distributed internationally by King Features Syndicate, Inc. For information, write to King Features Syndicate, Inc., 300 West Fifty-Seventh Street, New York, New York 10019, or visit www.KingFeatures.com.

Andrews McMeel Publishing, LLC
an Andrews McMeel Universal company
1130 Walnut Street, Kansas City, Missouri 64106

15 16 17 18 19 SDB 10 9 8 7 6 5 4 3 2 1

ISBN: 978-1-4494-7077-7

Library of Congress Control Number: 2015937250

Printed on recycled paper.

Mutts can be found on the Internet at www.muttscomics.com.

Cover design by Jeff Schulz

Thanks to Allyson Murphy, Taylor Jez,
Kyle Willie, and Stephanie Itle-Clark.

Made by:
Shenzhen Donnelley Printing Company Ltd.
Address and location of manufacturer:
No. 47, Wuhe Nan Road, Bantian Ind. Zone,
Shenzhen China, 518129
1st Printing — 7/13/15

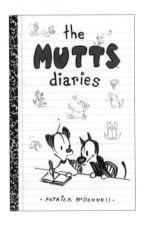
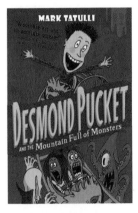

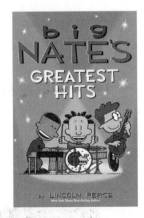